A WARRIOR'S STRENGTH

"I do not sing or pray for power." Daha-hen rode without turning around.

"Why not? The others say you are peculiar. Is it because you do not sing or pray?"

"I do not sing or pray because I am a man. There is power enough in that. A bundle of feathers that men can carry about or a stuffed owl cannot protect me or tell me what I will do. Only I can determine what I do." Daha-hen had found the words at last.

"That is peculiar."

"It is not peculiar," replied Daha-hen. "It is so."

"Still, it would be comforting to have the support of a greater force than one's self," Thomas Young Man spoke his thoughts.

"It is comforting to know your own strength and depend on it."

"What if you were without strength?"

"I am never without strength?"

"But what if you were wounded?" Thomas persisted.

"I have been wounded. I counted on myself."

"But what if you were so badly wounded, you could not count on yourself?" Thomas would not let go of the thought.

"Then I would die," stated Daha-hen.

"Are you not afraid to die?"

"No."

Other *Leisure* books by Cynthia Haseloff:
THE CHAINS OF SARAI STONE

MAN WITHOUT MEDICINE

CYNTHIA HASELOFF

LEISURE BOOKS NEW YORK CITY

Dedicated to
Whitney, Parker, and Brian

A LEISURE BOOK®

September 1999

Published by special arrangement with Golden West Literary Agency

Dorchester Publishing Co., Inc.
276 Fifth Avenue
New York, NY 10001

ISBN 0-8439-4581-8

Printed in the United States of America.

MAN
WITHOUT
MEDICINE

FOREWORD

The story of Daha-hen is a true story; at least the major incident in it is true. Big Bow, a Kiowa Indian, did go after stolen horses with a few rounds of ammunition, kill the horse thieves, and return to the reservation with his horses. Many of the minor incidents and people in the story are also real. The facts are there on the pages of history for all of us to read. But the feeling of the air coming off the Wichita Mountains, or the sound of the horses' breathing, or the thoughts and the feelings of the man are not written. These are now the truths of fiction.

Big Bow, or Zepko-eet-te, was a man of his time and culture. He was a brave man, an honorable man, and a man who killed without hesitation for self-preservation and, just as importantly, for status and social position among his own people. It is hard today to accept the honor in the killing creed of the Plains Indians. We try to gloss over it by saying the Indian was provoked by the rapacious whites who stole his land. But this is just not so. He killed for tribal status long before the white man came. He himself took the land of weaker Indians. The way of death was established early on — a conceit of the human heart that perhaps grew through unrestrained power and pride and only increased with the arrival of the horse, opening the Plains and the world to the Indian as never before.

The white man was a different enemy. He did not understand honor through blood. The white man's honor lay in the prolongation of life, even its material expansion, delaying the defeat of death. Even the white man's God defeated death, took it captive. The Indian's honor lay in the acceptance of death and defiance of defeat in death through bravery, by risking again and again the most precious trophy of life in a contest with other men who also knew the stakes and the risk. The Indian and the white man moved on the same board — the West. For the one life was an honorable game; for the other it never was. Before the Indian realized the stakes had changed from a brave life to the survival of a people, the game was almost over.

Big Bow and the other people of his generation experienced a cultural and psychic change that few of us know or even imagine. They went from lords of their world to government wards in a single lifetime. If we say that the white man was their persecutor and destroyer, the agent of genocide, we reduce them to victims. If we say that their tragic flaw, their defiant pride before or in the face of inevitable death, brought them down, we make them masters of their destiny, tragic figures far greater than any Hamlet or Othello.

It has always been hard for me to pity the Indian. He has been a great romantic figure to me — filled with greatness and with flaws, as are all great peoples and individuals. Mostly I have loved his greatness. But I have known his flaws. So this is not a politically correct or sensitive book. I have tried to make it accurate about the circumstances of 19th-century Kiowa culture and of Daha-hen's own life. If there are errors, I apologize.

It is not a story about a victim. It is a story about a man — a man who could stand on his own by comparison with any other man. It is a story about a man who knew the defining qualities of any honorable life — courage and hope and persistence and refusal to accept defeat through another man's definition of him.

Cynthia Haseloff
Springdale, Arkansas

Chapter One

Daha-hen saw the two specks when they first came over the horizon. He waited comfortably in the shade of the brush arbor. His white man's clothes lay neatly folded in the canvas teepee, discarded in the July heat. Today Daha-hen was a Kiowa as his father and grandfathers had been since the People knew themselves.

Daha-hen was not a young man. He was fifty-three. Old, some said, but Daha-hen had never listened much to sayings that found no truth in his heart. His copper body was as hard as it had always been since he was a grown man. The defeat and the thirteen years on the reservation had not caused him to lose the self-respect that tempered his life. He ate moderately, as he had always. He slept when he was tired, never exerted himself in the shimmering heat of the prairie day. He did not drink whiskey to forget who he was. He smoked in worship, not because tobacco was easy to get and cheap. Most of all, Daha-hen loved his horses, and they kept his heart young, full of hope. When he looked now to the west, he smiled, seeing colts and mares grazing the long rich grass. The horses were his and the Creator's who gave them into his care.

Fourteen years ago at Palo Duro the soldiers had shot the great Kiowa and Comanche horse herds. Remembering the screams of the dying horses still hurt Daha-

11

hen because the killing was of more than animals. The soldiers had been killing beauty and goodness and the life of the People. It hurt him because the horses were good animals and did not deserve to die. To kill a man's animals was to be small beyond measure. Daha-hen had lived that long day through with a conviction in his heart that his enemy might be strong and deadly, but he was not great as a man should be great.

And that conviction had followed him through the surrender, through the paperwork the white men substituted for thought. In his heart he had decided to live at peace on the land set aside. It had been time for that — too many of the People had died already. Daha-hen was a practical man, but he would not bow in his heart to the idea that the men who killed the horses were better men than he was. He knew they were not. He was in harmony with life on that subject — white men were wrong, out of step with the natural order of things, secure only in a world of their own creation.

Over the years Daha-hen had discovered the white men were out of step on many things. The clothes they issued on the reservation were stiff at first and too big, then the black color ran out and the clothes got smaller, and finally the thread and fabric itself acquired holes and fell apart. The food they promised did not come until the People were already hungry. And the soldiers said it was because of the paperwork. It was nobody's fault, they said, just the paperwork. Still the soldiers ate in spite of any paperwork. And Daha-hen had wondered at that. He had been a warrior himself, *toyapke* on many raids. He would have lost his self-respect if he had not cared for those he led above himself. He had talked with the other men.

"It is because we have no value," Old Man had said. He had thrown away his name because he was old and ready to die soon. "We are dust under their feet. We are now the prisoners, treated as we treated the captives when we were men." The other men looked at the ground, and Daha-hen had left them, angry in his heart. Even a captive must fight back. He knew that the ones who lived fought back, learned the ways, used them, but held their center.

The next morning Daha-hen had gone to the agent, not to ask again for food, not for blankets, but to say he was moving away to the edge of the reserve — away from the dead Indians, away from the paper men.

Headed for the edge of the reserve, his wife, Many Tongues, rode the mule that pulled their teepee and belongings. He rode the horse — shamefully, a mare so poor her bones showed, and the white men did not want her. He killed the mule under Scratching Rock where once the Osages had killed the Kiowas and put their heads in kettles.

"It is a sad place," Many Tongues said as she stood beside Daha-hen.

Daha-hen's black eyes lifted to the mountain. "Our people were afraid here," he said. "They tried to dig holes in the rocks to hide in. They scratched and dug at the rocks with their hands. But the earth did not hide them, and the enemy had no mercy. It is better to fight back than to be afraid."

Many Tongues thought of the dead ones beyond the hunger and cold, in the place of long grass and clear water. The buffalo had gone there, too. "To die is not so bad," she said, offering Daha-hen a piece of the boiled meat. "We are well acquainted there."

13

"We will live," said the man. "Every one of us will live."

"The People's medicine is gone," she said, looking at the sky and land.

"You grow forgetful, Many Tongues. You rode out long ago with Daha-hen, the Man Without Medicine," Daha-hen said. "We have gone many miles without owl prophets and bags of dog teeth and broken glass and prairie-dog skulls. It may be we will go a few more. We will see."

Daha-hen ate his food absently, watching the sick horse. He left the woman and went to the animal. Her neck was stretched out, her head nearly touching the ground. "We will see," he said, studying the desperate animal. He gathered brush for a fire and searched about for cedar, the sacred, healing bush. He built a small fire and lay the cedar on top. The horse did not resist as the Indian positioned her head above the rising smoke. Daha-hen took the blanket from his own shoulders and draped it over the horse's neck, trapping the smoke. He sat then in the cold, watching, thinking.

For many days Daha-hen tended the horse. Many Tongues stood with hands upon her hips and studied the horse as it ate the dry grass and mesquite beans she had gathered for it. They trapped prairie dogs and rats to feed themselves. Sometimes Daha-hen killed a rabbit or a 'possum. They did not grow fat, but they lived and grew strong and sure inside.

That first spring on the edge of the reserve the little horse ate the new grass. Daha-hen tied her out to draw the wild horses. He took ten horses in traps that spring. The bred mares he kept. The colts he and Many Tongues gelded and broke in the cold creek water.

That same spring cattle herds came north to graze

14

in the Indian pastures. Other Kiowas came from the agency and camped near Daha-hen to bargain for beef on the hoof from the Texans. Bellies of men and beasts were full in the time of good grass.

Daha-hen watched the cowboys, watched their quick little horses. When the Rancher came, he watched his movements, listened to the other men who traded with him. They said he was fair. Old Man had said the Rancher kept a herd of buffalo on his ranch and would not let them be hunted. Daha-hen had wondered, keeping the thought in his heart. Once, earlier, he had gone with men to get a buffalo for the annual sun dance of Kado. He watched the Rancher closely, considered him and the men around him. They were white, but not like the others he had known.

As a raider Daha-hen had traveled into the larger world beyond the Indian camps. He had walked the streets of Santa Fé with Mexican and white colleagues in illegal trade. He had known some well, like old Tafoya, the rich Comanchero who came to the Valley of Tongues. There many tongues, many languages were spoken. There stolen cattle and horses from Texas were traded for whiskey and repeating rifles and ammunition to kill other white men. The price was always too high — a cow for whiskey or *panocha* and *cemita*, wheat breads made by the Mexicans. A horse for a bolt of calico, fifty or more horses for a gun.

He also knew the old trader who made his living from the Navajos but easily betrayed them for a few horses. The old trader had once sent his son to guide Daha-hen to the sleeping Navajos for horses and scalps. The trader had provided Daha-hen with freshly saddled horses for his flight from the Navajos. Daha-hen had given the trader's son one of the three scalps he had taken on that raid. These were white men of the class with which Daha-hen had had contact.

He also knew the fighting or mewling ones he had killed — teamsters, surveyors, settlers, soldiers. When stripped of their clothes, they were ugly things, white as death except for turkey-red necks and faces and hands. Their covered-over backs and legs and arms had long, coarse, curling hair. Cut open these men possessed organs and muscles indistinguishable from any other man or beast. Even the brave ones' hearts were no bigger. But split open, they served to terrify other men. And split open, mutilated, they would never be whole in the after life. They would never fight again. That is what the People believed, but Daha-hen was not sure of it.

So Daha-hen watched the Rancher. When the Rancher's ponies grew thin with work, Daha-hen brought his ponies to him. He did not trade for cattle to eat but for gold coins and for two more mares with saddle sores and stiff legs.

With each spring there were more ponies in Daha-hen's herd. Each year he traded with the Rancher and his friends. Each fall Daha-hen got beeves, killed them, and Many Tongues dried the meat for the winter on frames in the sun. She mixed the pounded meat with nuts and berries, sealing it with tallow to make pemmican. Hides from the beeves were used to make moccasins and Many Tongue's dresses. Several times over the years the Rancher sent her a hide from a buffalo that had died. She prized these far above the cowhides. She worked them in the old ways. In the old ways she built cradleboards for the children she bore Daha-hen — new lives in the new time, new lives for the little ones lost. Her family was warm beneath the robes when the winds blew the northers against the lodge.

She wore a finely beaded robe when they went to the agency. Many Tongues was old-fashioned. She had little use for manta or calico. It was easily washed, easily fashioned, but bought at the high price of men's lives and the People's freedom. She used it sparingly. In fact, she took to few of the white men's goods except the iron cooking pot and ruffled parasol. Both had great usefulness.

At the agency Daha-hen's family still was eligible to receive issues of staples but found the trip long and the people near it desolate and quarrelsome. Daha-hen took what was given because he was a practical man and because the white men had agreed to give it. He kept his horse money and the grass lease money for the time when the supplies would not come because the paperwork was wrong.

Daha-hen and Many Tongues prospered on the edge of the reserve. They were not hungry even in the Moon When the Babies Cry for Food. Two children were born to them on Elk Creek where Daha-hen himself had been born in the Year the Stars Fell during the free time. Along Elk Creek far from white men and defeated Indians, sometimes it was like the free time again. But then, Many Tongues would remember how it had been in the camps, busy with life — children laughing, running, women talking, working, giving hides to make a young wife her first lodge. And Daha-hen, looking at the full moon, would remember the time he had brought home two hundred horses from Texas in one raid.

Horses. It was horses that made Daha-hen hope and live and prosper.

Daha-hen went inside and slipped the denim pants over his legs. His white shirt looked hot, but he put it on because the rider coming with his nephew, Elk, was a white man. White men made much of nakedness, gave it a shame in the Kiowas' eyes that had not been there in the free time. Daha-hen went back to the arbor, spoke softly to Many Tongues who gathered her sewing and went into the dark teepee. She did not like white people.

A breeze slipped capriciously beneath the arbor, touching Daha-hen's face and throat. Holding his sons who stood with their small arms around his neck, watching the riders, he thought: *It is a good life here. Many ponies, good grass, water.* Daha-hen was content.

Chapter Two

The Gambler, the white man who accompanied Elk, swung down, silver spurs jingling as his heels struck the earth. His horse's hoofs danced in the summer dust, stamping it with the print of iron shoes, newly set. Daha-hen observed the broad hat, split-tailed coat, two silver revolvers, brocaded vest, and waxed mustache that the Gambler sported. But it was the man's eyes he studied — colorless blue, darting about like waterstriders while Elk spoke of their meeting at Lone Wolf's camp.

"Uncle, we are going to play monte on a blanket in the shade of our arbor. Loud Talker and his sons are coming. We rode through their camp and herd and invited them," said young Elk.

Indians and cowboys sometimes gambled together with cards or on horse races. Neither had much to win or lose. But the Gambler who the boy had brought was no casual gamester.

"This one is not a cowboy," Daha-hen said.

Elk was eager for diversion. He had brought his uncle a gift. "He is unlucky," the boy said. "He lost five dollars to Lone Wolf this morning. Every Indian there took his money."

Daha-hen looked at the Gambler. While thinking, the Indian thrust his lower lip forward. He said nothing.

"Uncle, I have invited Loud Talker already," Elk repeated. "He is coming over the hill with his sons."

Daha-hen did not look in the riders' direction. He still watched the Gambler. He knew that life was not so convenient as to send gamblers who lost to Indians. Daha-hen did not believe in luck or medicine. He was not afraid of either. He would watch what happened.

"Tell Many Tongues, then," the elder Kiowa spoke. A game of monte would pass time pleasantly, and Daha-hen would teach his sister's son the dangers of the greater game of greed. "Decide before you begin where you will stop, Elk. A man's luck sometimes changes in a moment. You can ride it farther to see if it will change again but know where you will turn back."

And so they played. Sometimes the Indians won. Sometimes the Gambler took their money. They played through the long afternoon, through the long prairie twilight when the night sounds came, and into the moonlight by a bright fire. As the moon was setting, Daha-hen took his winnings, two new silver dollars. He walked to his pony and rode out to his herd. He did not see the Gambler's eyes as they followed him. The Gambler smiled and dealt the cards again.

When Daha-hen returned, he curled up in his blanket under the open teepee to sleep. Loud Talker and the Gambler played till dawn without disturbing his rest. The household still slept when they rode away together. Elk lay down, then, nearby. The men slept in the cool morning as Many Tongues ate breakfast and began sliding deer hide rhythmically back and forth across a pole, twisting the skin in her strong hands, softening it. She wished briefly that there were other women to talk with over the task but quickly remembered that too much talk would leave the task undone.

The morning passed, and neither Daha-hen nor Elk stirred. Sweat coated Daha-hen's body as he slept. At last he sat up slowly, too hot to sleep any more. He went down to Elk Creek for a while, bathed, and returned with the white man's overalls and shirt still rolled up under his arm. He went to the iron pot that held the day's food. He ate. At last he settled against the willow back rest and picked up the unfinished reins he was braiding. He yawned.

"Did Loud Talker win money?" he asked.

"He lost a horse," Many Tongues said.

"Hmm," said Daha-hen. "A horse." He braided the reins skillfully as he had learned long ago. "And our nephew?"

"He did not lose his horse," she said. "But his silver bracelet with the blue stones rode away with the white man."

"The Gambler's luck must have gotten better," Daha-hen concluded. The hobbled pony that Daha-hen kept for himself and Elk's roan stood under a mesquite, head to tail, amicably switching flies from each other's faces. Daha-hen yawned again and brushed a fly from his own face. When it was cool, he would go and check the herd that had grazed off beyond the rolling hill during the night.

And the afternoon passed as did the morning.

"Hey yup. Daha-hen!" Loud Talker rode toward Daha-hen's camp at a gallop. "Daha-hen. The white man . . . !"

Daha-hen could not hear the words. He stood up, watching Loud Talker waving frantically, and suddenly Elk was beside him. Loud Talker reined up in front of the two men. He was still waving and speaking very rapidly.

"My horses are gone. My horses are gone. Only this

21

one I ride remains. He came running into camp," said Loud Talker through his labored breathing.

Before Loud Talker finished, Daha-hen dropped the partially braided reins he held in his hand and went swiftly to the pinto he cherished. He released the hobbles and mounted. At the pressure of Daha-hen's knees the pony whirled and bounded up the hill. Elk, on the roan, was beside him.

Daha-hen's herd had been grazing all night in the rich grassland a mile from camp. Now his herd was gone, too. He rode, lying over the pony's spotted neck, reading sign. In moments the Kiowa found the trail. The direction of the herd changed, turning northwest. And there Daha-hen saw the iron-shoe prints in the creek sand — five hard-shod horses, five white men. Elk and Loud Talker along with Loud Talker's son and nephew, Broken Stick and Gnat Catcher, sat on the bank watching Daha-hen's tracking. At last he rode back.

"They came from the south. Five men." Daha-hen twisted on his pony, pointing the direction to the others. "One track I saw last night in my camp. The Gambler's horse is with the thieves. Go, Elk . . . all you boys go and see who else has lost horses." Elk turned and rode away, followed by Broken Stick and Gnat Catcher. "You and I will see where they went, Loud Talker."

The two warriors rode easily along the trail left by their herds and the thieves.

"They are white men," said Loud Talker, almost to himself. "We can do nothing against white men."

"They stole our horses," Daha-hen said.

"I only had a few head, not very good," Loud Talker noted. "Not so many as you."

"If it were one horse, I would want it," Daha-hen said.

22

"Even one horse is important now."

Loud Talker remained silent, feeling the rebuke for his gambling loss of one horse. At last he spoke, could not keep from speaking. "Your nephew brought this thief among us. He did not come to play cards, but to find our herds. Your nephew is foolish."

Daha-hen drew in his pony. "My nephew is still a boy. If anyone should have mistrusted this stranger, it was I. Do you quarrel with me, Loud Talker?"

Loud Talker sat in silence. He had ridden with Daha-hen on many raids. He knew the quiet warrior was deadly. His killing ways were swift and sure, untouched by hesitation or compassion once his mind was set. Daha-hen waited. "Then let us find this thief."

"We can do nothing," Loud Talker said.

"We can get our horses," answered Daha-hen.

"Very seldom has anyone ever gotten back stolen horses. The white men drive them off the reservation quickly. We cannot follow. We should not have made our camps so far from the agency. For two days, maybe three days, they would have been on our land if we had camped near the agency. Then we could have caught them and brought them to Agent Hall. Now they are gone. Our medicine is not good."

Daha-hen looked at the trail which cut west along the north fork of Red River. Across the river was Texas — the end of the Kiowa-Comanche-Wichita Reserve. All his life, as child, as man, he had ridden over the Plains. He knew each spring and creek for a thousand miles. But his knowledge was nothing now because he could not follow, could not cross the river without becoming an outlaw to be shot at whim by whoever happened to see him, could not cross because he had given up the old life, had promised to abide by the white man's ways.

"We must have a paper," Daha-hen whispered, surprising himself with the words. "If we have a paper, we can cross. We did it before to hunt. We will get a paper."

"By the time you go to Anadarko and get a paper and come back, those white men will have sold every horse and be gone. It is seventy-five miles there and seventy-five miles back. You are an old man now." Loud Talker looked at Daha-hen as he spoke. The other Indian did not look at him, did not seem to be listening to his words. "Maybe if you got there, Agent Hall would not even be there. Maybe he won't believe you or give you a paper."

"I will get a paper," Daha-hen said. "And I will get my horses."

Chapter Three

In the late afternoon Daha-hen left his camp at Sheep Mountain for the agency at Anadarko. Loud Talker and his son and nephew watched him ride off, then went to tell Lone Wolf and the others of their lost horses.

At first, as Daha-hen rode, he thought only of his horses and what he would say to Agent J. Lee Hall. He turned the idea many ways in his mind. He knew about horse thieves. He had been one of the best, never returning from a raid without at least one horse. The white thieves had taken his herd because it was the best, Loud Talker's because it was nearby.

He knew they planned to sell the horses. The Gambler was not a man interested in breeding or ranching. He was an easy-money man with regard only for his own profit. Daha-hen hoped that fact would cause trouble and delay among the other men. But he knew they were men of a kind who came together quickly for a purpose. Once it was accomplished, they as quickly separated. Even among Indians such groups joined and parted.

"Stay together," Daha-hen whispered. His mind added: *Take it slow. Fat horses show better. No stupid Indians can follow you. Take it slow. See the money,* tai-bos. *Now where are you headed?*

In the last glimmer of twilight Daha-hen walked the pinto, pacing it with the mastery of a lifetime. He let the horse drink from a shallow, tree-marked creek, splashed water on the slender legs, wet his own shirt, and wiped the back and sides of the animal. The coolness refreshed them both. And when he remounted, Daha-hen felt the eagerness of the pinto to push on. He smiled. It was a good horse he had raised and trained. Silently he stroked the damp neck.

The night was still and cool, a benediction for the day and his teeming thoughts. They walked in the enveloping darkness, waiting for moonrise. Daha-hen did not think about the distance ahead. All his life Daha-hen had ridden great distances. His legs were permanently shaped by the round bellies of countless ponies. Distance did not concern him nor did the prospect of riding alone. Many times he had been alone on the prairies, traveling deep into Mexico, as far as Tamipulas, and far out into the Rockies.

Once he had been gone three years — the time of his disgrace, the time he had learned to know himself, discarding the opinions of other men and the hope of any medicine. Among the independent Kiowa men, he had become the most independent, needing neither men's opinions nor men's conception of the ways of God.

Memories of the past came with the darkness, calming all the thoughts of Daha-hen's mind. He was at home in the emptiness. The power of his spirit renewed itself. In the silence he began to heal from the loud, troubling, fear-filled words of Loud Talker. The words had unsettled his usually calm and thoughtful center, teasing him with the defeated life around him. Niggling, uncomfortable words.

Once before he had fled from words he could not stop and the thoughts they had carried. He had fled then into the emptiness with only his shame and confusion. When he had returned finally, no man's words touched him again. He was no longer Zepko-eet-te, Big Bow, like his father and grandfather. He was Daha-hen, Man Without Medicine.

Young Man was not young, not to young Zepko-eet-te at least. He was forty years old, Zepko-eet-te eighteen. While the boy had been away on his second war party into Mexico, Young Man had taken Yellow Walking Woman as his wife. She was sixteen.

Zepko-eet-te looked at the horses he had brought back for her. There was no joy in them now. They were useless to him. The celebration sounds came across the night, proclaiming his victory and his great heartache. But he was bitter at the thought of his desire to bring the horses, at his childish joy and faith that, when he returned, her family would take the horses.

Her father and brother should have waited. He had told her brother he was bringing back horses for her. The brother had professed his friendship and agreed to carry his deeds before her father. But he had been false.

Brother and father both had smiled at Zepko-eet-te. But, while he was gone on the raid, they had given Yellow Walking Woman to Young Man for many horses and blankets and a gun. Her brother had taken the horses to their father's herd.

Zepko-eet-te could see the dark figures dancing near the fire. His mouth twisted. Liars. Betrayers. His own heart was good. His horses were good. But neither had had a chance — not a chance — in the face of their greed. He cursed himself for his trust. They had made him a fool, and he had helped them.

"Zepko-eet-te," a soft voice said near him.

He turned quickly. Before him stood Yellow Walking Woman. For moments he remained frozen by her beauty, by his own love for her.

"Young Man is good to me," she said. "Do not worry. He is prosperous. I am first wife, honored by him."

Zepko-eet-te blinked, wondering why she had come; why she had told him another man was good to her. Was she teasing him, making him small? He did not know these things.

She turned to go in his silence, then turned back her head, hurting the youth as no man had. There was a small tear on her cheek. "He is not Zepko-eet-te," she said and started away.

The boy broke, pain shooting through the center of his chest. He caught her and held her. She turned her face away. He forced it back. "You cannot go. I will not let you."

Still she pulled against his hold. "I said too much, Zepko-eet-te. I must go. Young Man is my husband, not you. He is a great warrior. He could kill me for coming to you."

Zepko-eet-te let her go back across the darkness to the fire, to the old warrior who had beaten him. The steady throbbing of the drums echoed the blood pulsing in his temples.

For days the boy sat in his teepee. His blanket covered his head. His mother brought food. He would not eat it. She built a fire. When she left, he kicked it out. She talked quietly to his father about him. Zepko-eet-te, Big Bow, the father was silent, but he looked at the smoke hole of his son's lodge from time to time. No smoke rose from a fire warming his son.

"It is his first defeat," he said aloud. "But every man

28

meets a defeat. Zepko-eet-te has strong medicine in war. He has been held high. At eighteen he is already a chief. He has thought himself better than other men. Some men here do not like his arrogance. Some men have resented him for his father and grandfather also. They are happy now. They wait to rush at him."

"A young man is sometimes tender about a woman," Zepko-eet-te's mother said.

"He must forget Young Man's woman, or he will be ridiculous. All he has accomplished will be as dust in the wind." His father set his jaw.

A father of a warrior did not lecture his son. A man had had his education. Big Bow had taught Zepko-eet-te many things, but he had not thought about women. He had not thought his son would be a fool for a woman. At last, Big Bow stood up. He wrapped the buffalo robe about his shoulders. Leaving the teepee, he walked straight to his son's lodge. He did not enter, but lifted the door cover.

"Zepko-eet-te," Big Bow said. "Uncover your head and hear one who speaks." Zepko-eet-te pulled the blanket from his face. He listened. His father and grandfather, whose names he now bore in turn, were men of honor and authority. They had never betrayed him. They had never been wrong for him. "Get up. Wash yourself. Go hunting. Be gone from this place until you are a man again." Big Bow went away, back to his own fire.

In a little while Zepko-eet-te emerged. He rode away without looking at the teepee where Yellow Walking Woman sat, sewing a shirt for Young Man.

Before sunset Zepko-eet-te hobbled his horse to graze and took shelter in an outcropping. He sat, silently looking at the late autumn landscape. He thought only of Yellow

Walking Woman. He was sure that she was not happy — not as he could make her happy.

On the fourth night Zepko-eet-te saw Yellow Walking Woman just as she had come to him at the horse herd. Silver earrings and the trade bells on the fringes of her deerskin dress jingled softly. The buffalo robe slipped off her lustrous hair. He heard her voice in the wind: "He is not Zepko-eet-te."

The boy reached out. The woman was gone. But her words came again and again. "He is not Zepko-eet-te," the young man repeated to himself. The thought grasped his mind. "He is not Zepko-eet-te." He stood up. "I only am Zepko-eet-te. He is not my equal." Zepko-eet-te whooped at the thought. "She is mine. Mine only. No man can stand against me. My medicine is strong."

In minutes he was down the hill. He stripped himself and plunged into the icy water. When he had bathed, he carefully dressed himself in his finery and braided long strips of otter fur into the single braid that hung beside his right cheek. He caught the horse, slipped the bridle over its head, and threw his saddle onto the sleek back. At last the young warrior rode back toward the village.

The first cold slashes of ice cut his face. He pulled his robe higher and rode into the rising wind.

Chapter Four

By the time Zepko-eet-te reached the village, snow covered the ground. Heavy wet flakes continued to fall, whirling with the wind into white dunes. The young warrior's wet eyelashes froze together. He rubbed them with his hand until he could see again.

Zepko-eet-te rode along the village street toward the teepee of Young Man. He passed his own small dark lodge and the lodge of his father. Smoke was rising between the ears of the yellow-striped teepee. Zepko-eet-te smelled the fragrance of his mother's cooking. He drew the aroma deeply into his senses. One day soon Yellow Walking Woman would cook for him, and his own lodge would be great among the lodges of the People.

Young Man's lodge had been painted. White circles dotted the blue-black of the hide covering. In his youth Young Man had dreamed that he would never be alone, that his medicine would see that he was always surrounded by the People. Even on a lonesome trail, the Seven Sisters would be with him, always.

Zepko-eet-te's mouth jerked slightly at the corners. It was not a dream, he thought. It was the story told of the seven Kiowa sisters and their brother who went out to play. The brother turned into a bear and chased the sisters who ran to a stump to get away. The stump, to protect them, began to rise in the air. Their bear brother

31

scratched the trunk, making deep marks as it rose mysteriously into the air. The stump became Devil's Tower, and the sisters became the stars of the Pleiades. All the Kiowas said they have kinsmen in the night sky.

Even Young Man's dream was nothing, *Zepko-eet-te* thought. His medicine was nothing, a retelling of an old story that belonged to all the People. To be always surrounded by the People, *Zepko-eet-te* thought contemptuously. Has Young Man no courage to be alone?

Zepko-eet-te guided his pony down the creek embankment and through the cold water. He rode out on the far side of Young Man's teepee, protected from the eyes of the People. Silently he slipped from the horse onto the snowy ground and lifted the teepee door.

Yellow Walking Woman was sitting across the fire from the door. The golden light of the flames were dancing over her face. She was beautiful.

"Your teepee is too close to the creek," *Zepko-eet-te* said. "An enemy could capture you and carry you away without anyone ever knowing."

"It is easy to get water from the creek," the woman answered. "I am not afraid."

"Gather your things and come with me. We will go away this night," *Zepko-eet-te* said without straightening.

The girl smiled and stroked her hair, with one hand, back behind her ear. The robe slipped from her naked shoulder. "It is snowing outside, but it is warm in here."

"Come now," the young man said, feeling the temptation of the woman and the fire. Looking about the lodge, he saw her saddle and bridle near the door. He reached out with his free hand and gathered them. "Bring only your own things that you brought with you to Young Man's teepee. Bring nothing he gave you. I will saddle your

32

horse while you do that. Come out to me when you are ready."

"It is snowing," the woman said again with a slight pout.

"The snow will cover our tracks." Zepko-eet-te dropped the door flap and returned to the horses. His heart pounded in his chest. The sight of her has done this, he thought, just the sight of her. To touch her, to lie with her. . . .

"You are smarter than that," the other voice inside Zepko-eet-te said. "You know that Young Man will come after her. He cannot permit you to steal his wife. He is a great warrior. He will lose the respect of the Kiowas if he lets you go. He must kill you."

"I am strong enough to stop him," Zepko-eet-te said as he had jerked the cinch of the woman's saddle tight. The horse grunted at the sudden constriction. "I am a warrior, too . . . younger, stronger."

"Older, wiser, more experienced," the voice inside whispered. "That's what Young Man is."

Zepko-eet-te slipped the bridle over the horse's head. "My medicine is strong."

"You are a fool, Zepko-eet-te," the voice said. "A dozen willing girls would go with you tonight and not bring an angry husband."

"This is the woman I want."

"You want this woman only because she belongs to someone else. He has already broken your medicine by taking her from you," the voice answered.

Before Zepko-eet-te could deny the voice, Yellow Walking Woman emerged from the teepee. The buffalo robe covered her shining hair and framed her small face with its fur. She smiled at Zepko-eet-te, and the

33

voice inside became mute.

The young warrior lifted the blanket from the back of his saddle. He dropped it over the woman and drew her to him. He breathed in her fragrance as he bent to kiss her.

"Since we are running away together, I will give presents to your family for our marriage," he said.

"It is not required," she said.

"It is not required." He tasted her lips again. "But I will do it anyway because I have power and because they have brought you . . . beautiful Yellow Walking Woman . . . into this world for me. My gratitude overcomes my contempt for their giving you to Young Man."

Yellow Walking Woman giggled and ran her fingers along Zepko-eet-te's lips. "You are sure of yourself."

"Yes," he almost shouted. "I am Zepko-eet-te, Big Bow, son of Big Bow who brought back his father's bones, son of Big Bow who rode to the far south country. What medicine I have that brings you to me! Come."

Zepko-eet-te lifted the woman into her saddle. She bent, and he kissed her again. He turned quickly and threw himself onto his pony. He nudged the animal forward, and the woman followed.

This time, going back into the shallow creek, he rode around the last teepees of the village. Finding a break in the bank, he led the woman out, and they skirted the main street of the village. They circled behind the firelit lodges.

"Why do you not ride down the very center of the encampment?" *the voice inside him asked.* "I thought your medicine was strong. You said you are strong and not afraid, but you are sneaking away with this woman."

Quiet! *Zepko-eet-te spoke the words to himself.* I am

34

not afraid, and I am not sneaking. I am a proven warrior. A warrior chooses the appropriate time and place for display at his own discretion. There is no one here to withstand me. One day I will confront Young Man.

The voice seemed quieted. One day we will see who confronts whom. Hmm, it sighed. What will you feed this jewel of a woman?

Zepko-eet-te sat up slightly on the horse. The snow was falling heavily, more heavily than before. It had become much colder now. No game would be found for days perhaps. He had with him only the scant food for a warrior to survive. He must think such thoughts as the voice had said. There was the woman to think of now and always.

Through the trees he saw the glow of his father's lodge. The ornamental yellow strips of cloth that usually danced from the long poles were limp and frozen. He nudged his pony toward the light. In the deep trees behind the lodge he dropped from his horse. He walked back to the woman, touched her leg as he stood beside her horse.

"You will wait for me," *he said softly through the whisper of the falling snow.* "I must get food for us."

Many years later, when Zepko-eet-te could bear to talk about it, Big Bow, his father, had told him fully of the night he had kept his son from Young Man's woman.

"Big Bow," *Feathered Lance said.* "I have seen your son tonight."

"He is well?" *asked Big Bow.*

"He rode down the center of the village to a lodge that is at the far end."

"Thank you," *said Big Bow. Feathered Lance withdrew from the door of the teepee.*

Big Bow was an ondai, the highest caste among the

35

Kiowa. The very word meant first or best. His own father had been ondai before him, but he himself had confirmed his high birth by his deeds. When his father, also called Zepko-eet-te, or Big Bow, was killed in the far-south country where the little men with long tails live in trees and speak no known language, he had gone after his father's bones and brought them home. He also had brought the scalps of four of those who lived in that country to avenge the death of his father.

His son, young Zepko-eet-te, had been a boy, dancing with the other young boys of the Polanyup, the Rabbit Society. In the dancing flames of the fire, Big Bow saw again the little boys dancing for him as they had on his return. His son carried a scalp as he whirled in the summer dust. The dust coated his small legs and feet.

Big Bow remembered the dust, remembered the intensity of the sweating child, honoring his father and grandfather. There had been a feast afterward for the boys. There were many feasts afterward, as the boy grew older, stronger, braver, more like his father and grandfather.

Now his son was a man, a toyapke, or pipe carrier, after only two raids, after only eighteen summers. Many older men recognized his skills and wished to ride with him on raids. But his son's interest was directed then only toward Yellow Walking Woman. Big Bow sighed and drew on his turkey-bone pipe, sucking the smoke of tobacco and sumac leaves into his throat and lungs.

He looked up from the flames into the black eyes of his wife, Sabiña. His mouth tightened. The woman spoiled the boy in inappropriate ways, coddled his softness. He expected she would want to yield to him regarding this woman, this pretty Yellow Walking Woman.

"Woman, speak what is in your heart," Big Bow said.

"This is not the woman for our son," Sabiña said straightly.

Her answer puzzled Big Bow. "You worried before because he pined for her and would not eat."

"I worried before for his grief, for his tenderness over the woman. I did not want him to have her."

"Because she is Young Man's wife?" asked Big Bow.

"Because she is lazy and selfish. Because she glances sideways at many men." The mother stirred the coals of her cooking fire.

The man dropped his head to his chest. The woman was not worried about the mature husband-warrior's anger. "You do not want her for the mother of your grandchildren?"

"No." Sabiña spoke softly. "There are better wives for our son. He could never satisfy or trust that one. There will always be strife over that one."

"You are established on this thought, even if Young Man could be appeased and compensated?"

Sabiña nodded. "But let it be his choice . . . give him time to see her."

Big Bow tossed the pipe, burned out, on the dirt floor before him. "How am I to do that? You want his father to stop him and save his pride at the same time."

"Not his pride, my husband," she said. "His heart. He is not thinking with his head."

"I know what he is thinking with," the father said.

"It is not like that with him," Sabiña added quickly. "He does not just want her . . . he holds her up. He dreams dreams."

"Of what?" puzzled Big Bow. Of what, if not warm flesh and pleasure? he thought.

"Of gallant ways," she said. "He rescues her. He rides,

37

a defiant warrior against the injustice of her family and her husband."

"I do not understand this," Big Bow said.

"You do not understand this," Sabiña affirmed.

Big Bow sat, looking at the fire. "He rescues her? How? From what? Her husband is rich and honored. Her family is gifted well for her. What injustice?"

"Think as a boy of eighteen summers," Sabiña said.

"He is a man, proved in war, toyapke, leader of men."

"You have taught his mind and body the ways of war. But his heart has escaped your notice. He is a boy of eighteen summers with great visions of himself."

"I have made him a man, a warrior." The father stuffed the words with the dried leaves into the pipe he had picked up. "He knows better than this. Everyone will think he is silly." The last word tasted strange in Big Bow's mouth. He had never used or even thought it before about his son.

"Everyone else sees her as she is. He sees her through his heart, through his dream," Sabiña said. "You must delay him, until the dream clears, and he sees as others see."

Big Bow stuck the pipe into his mouth and lit it. "He must come here when he remembers he needs food to feed her, and he cannot get it himself in this storm." He drew on his pipe. "He will not leave without seeing his father. He will not leave with that woman this night. That is what I say."

Big Bow, the father, sat comfortably on the north side of his fire, the place of honor in any Kiowa teepee. He smoked contentedly from the turkey-bone pipe. He had no need tonight for the long-stemmed pipe that warriors shared as they told stories and considered strategies.

38

Across from him Sabiña held her bead work near the fire as she decorated a buckskin shirt. She looked up, not at the noise made by her son, for he was silent upon his entrance, but at the cold air that rushed in before him. She caught her breath at the bad sign, the cold that the boy brought with him.

"Welcome, my son," Big Bow said. "Come and sit by the fire and warm yourself. It is a night for long tales of great deeds. I want my son here beside me for I am lonely for the warriors who have gone."

"Father," the young warrior said, "I need food for travel."

"You shall have food, my son. In your whole life, have I kept any good thing from you? Have I not favored you, spoiled you, loved you with all my heart?"

"Yes, Father. I have wanted for nothing in your household," the young man of eighteen summers answered. He sat beside his father. There was no man, except his dead grandfather, he honored or respected more. The respect had been carefully taught to him as a principle of the People, but it grew even more deeply out of his heart's knowledge of his father and grandfather.

"Bring the pipe, woman," Big Bow said. "Sit with me, talk with me, listen to my heart, my beloved son. It is as cold as the snow, as lonely as the searching winds. You are just what my heart needs tonight, my son. When you are a father yourself, you will have thoughts of love for your son that I have for you."

Sabiña handed the long pipe to her husband and glanced into his eyes.

"Your grandfather was ondai before me, a great man," his father continued. "Men in that time were stronger, better men than we are now. They were just taking to the horse, discovering the life we lead. Think to have

39

gone from a man on foot to a man who rode to the great forests to the south! He made that journey twice. I made it once . . . to bring back his noble bones."

The young warrior's attention drifted toward the door, the snow, the woman beyond. Big Bow saw and drew him back with his words. "Do you remember when you danced as a rabbit for your grandfather? You carried one of the scalps I had brought back."

"Yes, Father," the boy said. "I remember grandfather."

"I will tell you of a great raid your grandfather took," Big Bow said, drawing on the long pipe. He blew smoke softly to the sky, the earth, the other directions. Then he handed the pipe to his son who likewise blew the sacred smoke to all the directions as the father silently watched. "Your mother knows this story, but I am not sure I have ever told it to you. He was a very handsome man, your grandfather. You are much like him. Many women sighed and glanced sideways when he rode by as they do for you." He laughed softly.

Zepko-eet-te smiled a small smile but could not look up from the fire.

"His leggings had fringes that touched the ground from horseback, and Mexican silver hung from his ears and chest."

"Is this a long story, my father?" asked the young man softly, thinking again of the woman waiting outside.

"Oh, yes, my son. This story will last us the whole night because there are many side stories that flow into the main story." Big Bow blew smoke into the air, filling it with the tobacco's fragrance. "Sit back, my son. This story is very satisfying. It is also your story because it is the story of your grandfather. Sabiña, bring a robe for our son and food to eat while we talk. Pack meat also for his journey when we are finished."

The son could not stop the father. He loved him, respected him, and honored him too much. He could not disrespect this great warrior, this beloved father. The teachings and habits of his life were too strong. His own will and the woman must wait.

The first light of day colored the winter sky when the last of Big Bow's story was finished. The snow had stopped. The winter stars were yet bright in the black canopy. He sighed contentedly. "Sleep, my son," he said at last.

"I must go, Father," the boy said.

"Yes, my son, you must go," said Big Bow. "Give him the food, Mother. Our son has far to go and will need much food if he goes into the far-south country like his grandfather and I have."

"That is where I am going, Father. Thank you, Mother, for this food and moccasins." Sabiña had filled a second parfleche with clothes for her son, including several pairs of moccasins.

The young warrior stepped out into the cold demi-night and waded through the deep snow back toward the horses. His horse was still tied, but Yellow Walking Woman and her horse were gone. Zepko-eet-te dropped the pouches he carried in the snow.

He frantically began to read the signs around him. A third horse had come into the trees and turned about several times. There were hoofprints. The young man's heart raced. The woman had been carried away by enemies. He read, searched, turning in the snow. Then he saw that the trail did not go back along the perimeter of the camp or off into the open country. It turned straight into the main village street.

41

The boy caught his horse and rode after the tracks. Noises from the other end of the camp caused him to pull up. He could see women outside Young Man's teepee. He also saw the warrior's horse and pack animal tied beside Yellow Walking Woman's pony.

Zepko-eet-te rode slowly toward the blue-black teepee. Carefully, smoothly, he drew the bow from his quiver, strung it, and fitted an arrow onto the sinew string. The pony walked steadily, ears alert, until he pulled it to a stop with his knees.

Zepko-eet-te called out: "Young Man, send out Yellow Walking Woman. Do not hold her. It is her will to go with me. I will take her from here."

Young Man emerged into the first clear cold light. Women went past him into the teepee.

"You, Zepko-eet-te, great warrior, son of warriors, little Big Bow." Young Man's scornful words rang in the crystal air. "You have no honor. You have stolen my wife and let her feet freeze. How could you be called a great warrior when you cannot even protect a stolen woman from the cold? Behold, this warrior, my friends, he is a tiny baby who takes what is not his and has it taken away. Will he cry loudly for his father or will his mother's milk quiet him?"

In the periphery of his vision Zepko-eet-te caught the shape of his father, naked to the waist from quick rising, shield over his bare hard arm, lance in his hand.

"Will you fight me, Big Bow, and save this mewling pup from my wrath?" asked Young Man, reaching for the lance beside the door.

Big Bow did not answer the warrior. "I am beside you, my son," he said softly to Zepko-eet-te. "Where you lead, I will follow."

Zepko-eet-te rode forward, drawn by his love and concern for Yellow Walking Woman and by the horrifying words of Young Man. The horse picked its steps slowly in the snow.

"Is she dead?" he asked.

"See for yourself, boy," said Young Man, stepping aside.

Zepko-eet-te dropped to the ground and looked inside Young Man's lodge. Two women were bathing Yellow Walking Woman's feet and rubbing the toes. Other women stood watching. Yellow Walking Woman looked up at Zepko-eet-te.

Her voice was very clear as she spoke to the women. "Zepko-eet-te is not Young Man and will never be such a fine man. He is a baby, unable to leave his father and mother. What woman would want such a child? I was right to have chosen Young Man. Zepko-eet-te has no medicine."

The other women laughed. Zepko-eet-te withdrew his head and shoulders and lowered the door covering. Blood pounded in his ears. Zepko-eet-te is not Young Man. He could see the laughing faces around him. Women, children, warriors were laughing. Young Man was laughing with them. Zepko-eet-te could see the laughing, but he could not hear for the blood pounding, for the words kept echoing: Zepko-eet-te is not Young Man. Zepko-eet-te has no medicine. What good were his weapons against such words and laughter and shame?

He let go of the door covering and turned. He did not look at Young Man as he walked to his horse and quickly mounted. His eyes were on the horizon as his legs moved the horse back and away. Zepko-eet-te rode past his father who still stood bow in hand in the center of the village street. He rode past his mother who stood beside the lodge with her hands over her lips. He rode alone away from the People toward the far-south country.

Chapter Five

Daha-hen breathed deeply of the cool night air. It was a long time ago that he had ridden into the far-south country — thirty-five years before — a lifetime, a lifetime of change. Now he was not the Kiowa who took horses from white men. He was the Kiowa whose horses had been stolen by white men. And he, the once free-roaming raider, must now have a slip of paper before he could leave the reservation to seek those horses. An agent of the United States government that he had fought against for so long must now approve his comings and goings. The night was far gone when he crossed the familiar roll of land that led to the river and toward the agency.

The Anadarko Agency lay on the road between Fort Sill and Fort Reno. From it the agent oversaw the 4,256 people, what was left of the Comanche, Kiowa, Kiowa Apache, Wichita, and Caddo nations. Their communal reserve consisted of almost three million acres.

The Comanches, most powerful and numerous of the peoples, pitched their teepees along the Little Washita, southwest of the agency. Along Elk Creek and Rainy Mountain Creek, west of the agency, a thousand Kiowas lived in the dirty canvas lodges that had replaced their beautiful, painted, buffalo-skin dwellings. The few remaining Wichitas, Caddoes, and Kiowa Apaches, descimated now by warfare and disease, lived in the center of the agency along Cache Creek.

To the east was Fort Sill. A few tribesmen camped there for the convenience of the post store. Quanah Parker's Comanches had pulled up stakes and moved to Cache Creek when Lieutenant Colonel John Davidson replaced Colonel Grierson. That was a long time ago. Quanah was friends now with the big ranchers who wanted the Indian grasslands to graze their cattle.

The Indian nations were all different now, Daha-hen thought. Many of the People found living near the whites to be useful. Many camped around the agency itself to be close to the ration dispensary. Sometimes their children went to the school. Sometimes the People themselves went to the mission churches that functioned there with traveling preachers. They liked the stories and the singing, they said. The Methodists were most excellent singers.

Daha-hen let the horse drink before riding further. The Washita, with its quicksand bottom, ran through the agency, watering the cattle that grazed the long bluestem grass. It was good grazing country, Daha-hen reflected, good for horses, good for cows, too. The Washita no longer mingled the blood of Indians and white men in its moving waters. The water was clear and fresh, but muddy with memories, if a man stopped to watch as he watered his horse.

In the valley of the Washita, when he was a young man, Daha-hen had seen the forty-two skeletons of the Cheyenne Dog Soldiers that Satank and the Kiowas had massacred for intruding into their country. They had found and trapped the soldiers and killed each one to the very last. They had taken their scalps but had left the bodies and their possessions untouched to honor

45

their valor. It had been excessive to have killed them all, but Satank was a crazy man.

At Beaver Creek, in the watershed of the Washita, Big Bow, his father, had fought the Cheyennes who had come to avenge the murder of their people. The battle had lasted all day long. Many had died — women digging for roots beside the stream, warriors trying to catch their ponies. Many men had died in displays during the fighting. Many children had been left. It had been bad. Everyone said that it had been bad. That had been the last fight with the Cheyennes. There had been enough killing. The Kiowas, Comanches, Cheyennes, and Arapahos had made peace in 1840.

When they had sat down in council in the Cheyenne country, Eagle Feather of the Kiowas had said that they had brought back the heads — that's how the old men talked of scalps — of the forty-two slain Cheyenne Dog Soldiers. They were wrapped carefully in a blanket. High-Backed Wolf, speaking for the Cheyennes, had lifted his hand to stop the opening of the bundle. "Friends," he had said, "to show and to talk about these things will make for new bad feelings. We have peace. Let us continue to have peace. If I saw my son's hair, I would forget peace. You take away these heads and use them as you think best with regards to our friendship. But do not let us see them or hear of them. They touch our hearts too deeply."

"You have spoken well," Tohausen, a Kiowa chief, had said. "Pick a place where we shall come to meet you. Make it a wide place for we have large camps and many horses. We will give you many horses. There in that wide valley we will make a strong friendship between our peoples. It will not be broken. It will last forever."

46

That had been when Daha-hen was a child. He had been the witness child. Gifts had been piled high around him. He had seen the chiefs speak. He had witnessed the peacemaking. As long as he lived he would remember. He would tell those who came after. The peace would not be forgotten.

That was the way Indian peoples made peace — when there was enough killing, enough crying. But there was never enough with the whites. The People could not bring them to that. There were always more white men. So they had brought the Indians to that. There had been enough killing of their own people, for the Kiowas. But the peace was not satisfying as it had been among Indian peoples. They were never on equal terms with the white men. The white man always maintained the whip hand. His gifts were not freely given. They were bribes intended to buy the People. And the white man had no use for people who sold themselves for blankets and rations.

Daha-hen watched the water of the clear Washita sliding away beneath the horse's lips. This river had seen much. Daha-hen had once ridden to the big bend of the Washita and seen where General George Armstrong Custer and the Osage Wolves had killed Black Kettle's Cheyennes in 1868. Satanta had shown him where the Kiowas and Cheyennes from the lower camps had caught Major Joel Elliot and his men — cut off from the battle — and had killed them and had mutilated their bodies. Custer had never come to help them or to find them. He had run away because he had known the other Indians were coming. *Custer had been no man*, thought Daha-hen. A *toyapke* did not leave his men or his wounded. But Custer was dead now, and he deserved to be dead.

Satanta was dead, too, now. He had jumped to his death from the hospital floor in the Huntsville prison in Texas where he had been returned to serve out his sentence for the murders of the freight-wagon men. The white men had put him back there after the Wrinkled Hand Chase had violated the terms of his parole. The fighting outbreak at Anadarko had begun the flight. The white men had pursued the Indians for more than a month, west from Anadarko toward Palo Duro, west into their stronghold. There were some good fights for the young men — the Lyman supply train, the buffalo wallow — but it had really been a long, dying chase. It had been raining then, raining and raining, until the Indians' hands had become wrinkled from the water. So the Wrinkled Hand Chase became the end of all the fighting. There had been nothing left — no places to hide, no buffalo to eat, no horses to take them away, no will to continue fighting what could not be fought. The People could not get Satanta out that time, and he could not stand being in the prison. They — white and red, great men and cowards — were only dust now on the ever-moving prairie wind. The Washita still moved on, its face wrinkled only by the rocks that occasionally broke its smooth surface.

The agency at Anadarko was dark when Daha-hen walked his pony along the dusty street toward the picket-fence yard of the agent's new brick house. The fires, burning in the teepees scattered around the agency, were low, barely illuminating their silhouetted poles and sleeping people. He passed by the old agent's house, used when the Quakers were in charge in the 1870s. Poles along one side of the frame building braced its

48

bowed side, preventing collapse. *The old teepee poles held up the white man's building pretty well,* Daha-hen thought with a small smile. Not everything white men did in this country worked so well.

But the new agent had a brick house, solidly built, with materials freighted from the railroad terminal at Henrietta. He was a different man from the others. J. Lee Hall was called Eck-hob-it Paph, or Red Head by the Comanches; the Kiowas' name for him was Aycufty. Whichever language, the outwardly distinguishing features of the tall thin agent were his red hair and sweeping handlebar mustache. It was a change.

The man, J. Lee Hall, was different in other ways from the former agents. He was younger, more energetic. He had been a marshal and a Texas Ranger. He was not afraid to fight. This fact was not lost on the warriors. He had single-handedly, in his shirt-sleeves, grappled Lone Wolf — who had defied the previous agents and the Indian police and bullied the other Indians — to the ground, tied him up, and lifted him by the seat of his pants into the back of the buckboard. In the process he had relieved the chief of two revolvers, and not one shot had been fired.

Hall was not afraid to fight, but he was strong enough to reason with the Indian men as men. When deputy marshals from Texas had come with warrants for Ka-ma-ta and Po-tan-te, Hall had called the men to his office and detained them. When they had attempted to leave, drawing pistols from their belts, he and his clerk had forcibly disarmed them. However, the unarmed Indians had managed to break for the door and escape into the hot September air. In their haste they had passed the Texas marshals, knocking them aside with the force of their passage. Hall had held his fire. At the gate Kiowa men had tossed the fleeing warriors Winchesters, and they had turned to fire on the marshals and Hall. But the look in the ex-Ranger Captain's eyes and the leveled pistols in his hands had caused them to drop their guns and flee toward their teepees. In moments the agency building was then surrounded by a hundred armed Indians ready to defend their brothers, ready to kill the few white men. Hall had ordered the marshals and his staff inside the fragile building. They had waited.

At last old Stumbling Bear, who had fought in every Kiowa battle from the 1850s until he took the peace road in 1872, had made his way to the steps of the building. Hall had met him on the porch. They had talked, sat down together, and talked more. Once Stumbling Bear had seemed to laugh. When he had stood up to leave, Stumbling Bear had known that the two Kiowas had forfeited the protection of the tribe by stealing horses in Texas and subjecting them all to punishment. He had known "Red" Hall meant for the two to pay for their offense. He also had known that Hall meant to put an end to the thieving of the Indian horses by Texans. Texas thieves had caused the retaliatory raid by the Kiowas. Rolled barbed wire and fence posts, stacked around the agency yard, had born him silent witness. Stumbling Bear had left. And in a little while the men surrounding the agency had followed him. Kama-ta and Po-tan-te had left with them, but Hall had made the arrests later without incident.

Hall was different in other ways, too. He was an optimist about the Indians. He believed they were human beings who could learn new ways and make good lives

50

for themselves. He had been a teacher when he had come to Texas from North Carolina. He became a teacher again, making assignments on Monday morning, checking on the children and their missionary teachers during the week. He said more Indian children would live if the food was better. He bargained with the cowmen to pay their grass lease money in heifers so the Indian herds would grow, and there would be food always.

When Hall's wife and little girls had come to the agency, he took them into the lodges of the People. He explained to his family what the People were doing as they worked. He touched the smooth buckskin to the girls' pink cheeks. "Soft, beautiful," he said, and smiled. Then he said it again in Kiowa to the children, teaching them. Many Tongues had heard it. Many Tongues said Agent Hall was a good white man.

When Mrs. Hall lit the first light inside the new house this morning, Daha-hen was sitting on the porch beside Emmor Harston, the interpreter. The door swung open and Lee Hall, still in his socked feet, invited the men inside. His suspenders hung about his hips as he led them into the office.

"You're here early, men. What's the problem, Daha-hen?" He sat on the edge of his desk. Emmor translated.

"I have come for a paper," Daha-hen said to Emmor.

"What kind of paper?" The agent studied the Kiowa's face.

"To leave the reservation and go after my horses," the Kiowa answered through Emmor.

Hall settled back. He observed Daha-hen closely. The Kiowa's face was stripped of eyebrows and all other hair except a fragile mustache at the corners of his mouth.

Daha-hen was an old-time Indian in the way he wore his hair — one wrapped braid on the left, the right side cut short so as not to interfere with his bow hand.

"Your horses were stolen by white men?" asked Hall.

"Yes," said Daha-hen.

"How do you know?"

Emmor spoke what Daha-hen told him. "A gambler came to their camp, day before yesterday. Daha-hen recognized his horse's tracks among the other iron-shod horses that drove away his herd. He followed them to the river . . . saw where they crossed."

"Well," Hall said, getting up slowly, "that's more than seven hundred horses stolen in three years. Damn' Texans. They'd holler like hell if the Kiowas started raiding again." He walked to the map on the wall behind the desk, stuck his finger on the reservation, then on Texas. Anyone could see the proximity of Texas to the reserve. A thin wandering line — Red River — marked the flimsy natural boundary.

"How long ago?"

"Yesterday afternoon," the interpreter continued. "He started out right after, late yesterday."

"He just rode seventy-five miles here to get a paper so he could go after the horse thieves?" The agent turned to Emmor Harston. The interpreter nodded.

Hall knew Daha-hen's history. The Kiowa, who stood before him, had been with the raiders that executed the massacre on the Warren wagon train. He'd been in on killing the Abel Lee family and countless others. During the Wrinkled Hand Chase, he'd hit the Lyman wagon train, carrying Colonel Nelson Miles's supplies. He, along with a hundred Comanches and Kiowas, had pinned the train down for four days, without water, before a

52

relief column had delivered the soldiers from certain death. Many among the Kiowas regarded him as the most deadly of a deadly people. Daha-hen was not all blow like Satanta — he was just a killer, a cold, steady, remorseless killer. And yet, since giving his word to Kicking Bird, he'd kept the peace.

"Seventy-five miles in the wrong direction to keep his promise not to leave without permission. Would a white man do that? Hell, no." "Red" Hall walked around behind his desk and opened the drawer. "You tell him he's got the paper." The man sat down and began to write as Harston translated.

"Captain, there's something else," said Harston. Hall looked up. "He wants to know what he can do if the white men put up a fight?"

Hall laid the pen down and looked into the Indian's black eyes. "You tell him, if they shoot at him, I said he can shoot back to defend himself. But he's not to fight under any other circumstances. Clear?"

Harston translated, and Daha-hen nodded his agreement to the terms. Captain Lee Hall, one-time marshal, one-time Texas Ranger, folded the paper, creased it, and handed it to the Indian.

"Watch yourself, Daha-hen. I learned a long time ago in Texas a horse thief can't be trusted."

The white man walked to the door with Daha-hen. Agent Hall started to put his hand on the warrior's shoulder but satisfied himself by saying again: "Watch yourself. I'll ride out and see the horses when you get back. Maybe we'll string some wire."

Daha-hen walked down the path and through the fence alone, as Agent Hall and Emmor Harston went back inside. He went to where he'd tied the horse to graze and found a boy sitting on its back.

"Get down," he said.

The boy crossed his arms over his chest.

"A man does not get on another man's horse. Where were you raised, Rabbit?"

"You are an old man," the boy said. "You can't make me get off this horse if I want to sit on it."

Daha-hen stepped to the horse's head. "You think not . . . ," he began, and with one swift move he pulled the boy to the ground, jerked him up, and shoved him away. "Go home, Rabbit. I do not have time to teach a petulant boy respect for his people."

Daha-hen led the horse away into the street and back toward the river. "I thought a man always rode," the boy said contemptuously as he walked after the warrior.

"A man always takes care of his horse, Rabbit. This horse has come a long way, and he must go a long way more before he goes to work."

"You are Daha-hen," the boy said. "I have heard of you."

Daha-hen did not answer but walked on. The boy continued to follow. "My father rode with you," he said.

"What is your father's name, Rabbit?"

"Young Man was my father. I am called Thomas Young Man. That is what I am called by the Methodists." The boy strode beside him.

"You have your father's name." Daha-hen walked on with the boy at his shoulder. "Your father was killed at Palo Duro Cañon in the Wrinkled Hand Chase. That is fourteen years ago. You must have been unborn then."

"I was born. I am fifteen," the boy said.

"Where is your mother?" Daha-hen asked, thinking for the first time in many years of Yellow Walking Woman.

54

"She is a drunken whore at the fort with the soldiers," came a voice from off to the side. It was Old Man, sitting at the side of his teepee where he had just finished his morning prayers. "This one," he said, pointing at Thomas Young Man, "is thrown away . . . a *dapom*. The missionaries have taken him up, but they have not been successful."

Daha-hen considered the boy. His hair was short like all the missionaries' boys, like a white man. He had on a tattered kind of uniform jacket and dirty Levi's. On his feet were the remnants of moccasins. Too many boys were like this one, skinny, hungry for more than food. No one had enough left inside to feed them — not even their fathers or mothers.

"Old Man," Daha-hen said, looking away, "do you still have a rifle?"

"Yes, I have it," the ancient one answered.

"I have need of a gun," Daha-hen continued his thought. "My wife will give you a blanket for the use of this gun and cartridges."

"I do not loan cartridges. When they are used, they are gone," Old Man said. "You will have to pay money for the cartridges."

"I did not bring money, Old Man. If I had money with me for cartridges, I would go to the store."

"I have cartridges I will give you," Thomas Young Man offered as part of the exchange. "But I will need my rifle."

"Very well," said Old Man. "You may take my rifle, Daha-hen, and this worthless boy can give you cartridges." The old one went into his lodge, leaving the two outside. They heard him speaking to his wife, searching for the battered old gun.

"The Methodists let you have a gun?" asked Daha-hen.

"They like rabbit stew, and I am a good shot," the boy said.

"Go and get the cartridges. I will wait at the river after Old Man gives me the rifle."

As the horse browsed the sweet-smelling grass, Daha-hen thought about the boy bringing cartridges. An orphan boy in the old days could make a place for himself through raiding. With no value to his life, he did not mind risking himself. Some orphans, Mexican and white captives even, became important men. It was rare, but it could be done. Quitan had done it with Daha-hen's help. He had even given the Mexican warrior his sister for a wife; Daha-hen could count on Quitan.

Just two or three good men, maybe one who spoke Spanish, were enough for a successful raid, Daha-hen thought to himself. Large parties of a hundred, like Satanta led, were awkward, hard to manage, given to owl prophets and show. Daha-hen had ridden with Satanta.

The Corn Train Fight — called the Warren Wagon Train Massacre by the white men — was a perfect example. A hundred men had been on that raid, many little more than this boy, and an owl prophet, Mamanti, to be consulted and paid for propitious signs for the attack, for personal forecasts of victory or defeat that made foolish men brave and brave men foolish. The Kiowas had hit the wagons just after noon, watching the thunderstorm rising, knowing it would hide their tracks and allow them to return to the agency without pursuit. They had killed a mule in the last wagon's team before the driver could close the circle and secure a barrier against the attackers. The young men had been eager. Full of brave visions they had been hard to hold.

Gunshot, little older than this boy, had broken away,

run to a wagon, and had counted coup. Before he could return, he had received a bullet point blank in the face. But he did not die — not then. The bullet had torn off the side of his jaw, ripping open the interior, streaming blood. All order had collapsed, then. Many men had swarmed the wagons, killing men, seizing axes, hacking wagons to pieces and men, too.

Gunshot and some others had seized his assailant and hung him with chains on a wheel, head down, and had built a fire under his head. When his screams had become too much, while yet he lived, Gunshot had cut out his tongue. The boy had laughed and joked at the man's agony, satisfied for his own soon-approaching death.

But while the herd of warriors had spent themselves, white men had escaped and hidden in the timber. Dahahen had gotten one, but had quit at last from trying to get the others, irritated by the chaos among the Kiowas. One of the teamsters had gotten to Fort Richardson and had brought the soldiers upon them as never before.

So much for big raids and owl prophets, thought Dahahen. Satanta, on the Mamanti's advice, had let the first party pass and waited for another. The raid had seemed very successful — seven whites killed and forty-one mules taken. But they had been wrong. The first party had contained the white war chief, William Tecumseh Sherman. Alive and realizing not only his own miraculous escape, but the true Indian danger, Sherman had made war. Sherman had made war like no other white man. He had killed everything — men, buffalo, horses. When Satanta had boasted in his face of leading the raid, Sherman had turned him and those he named over to the Texans for trial. They had wanted to hang Satanta but sent him to prison instead.

What if that owl prophet had let them kill Sherman, as he had passed by? Would the Indian peoples still be making war on the white men? Would there still be buffaloes for the People? Daha-hen did not care to speculate. He had fought enough. He bent his face to the water and splashed its coldness into his eyes.

Thomas Young Man trotted his skinny pony among the teepees of the Kiowa camp, past the trader's store and the agency building, along the dry hard-packed street toward the river. Across his pommel he carried his rifle. The cartridges were in his pocket. A blanket, a small bag of jerked meat, and a water gourd were tied to the cantle. He found Daha-hen, as he had said, beside the river.

Daha-hen looked into the young face of the thrown-away boy. "Do you have the cartridges?"

The boy reached into his pocket and withdrew his hand. He opened it in front of Daha-hen's eyes. "There," he said. In his outstretched hand lay seven cartridges. Daha-hen looked up into his face. "You may have one."

Daha-hen took one. "Thank you very much, Thomas Young Man."

The boy closed his hand. "That will be enough if you are the great warrior people say you are."

Daha-hen pulled his horse's head up and tightened his girt. He put his moccasined foot into the stirrup and swung up. Without a word he moved the horse into the still-dark river and across to the other side. Thomas watched them go over the rise and out of sight, then pushed his own pony into the water.

Chapter Six

Daha-hen stepped out of the brush and caught the horse's rope and twine bridle. "Why are you following me?" he asked.

"Because you are going somewhere," answered Thomas Young Man.

"I do not ride somewhere with children. You go back to the Methodists. It may be that they will be successful with you." Daha-hen stood with his hands on his hips. "Out here you will die, like the boys who ran away from the school and froze."

"It is not winter now. I will not freeze," the boy said.

Daha-hen sighed. "Summer is dangerous. The land is dangerous. You know nothing. I saw you when you crossed the river. I will switch you and your horse and send you back." He lifted his quirt and tested its flexibility.

The boy, Thomas, sat without expression, watching the man. "Do you think I have not been beaten before? I have been beaten and run off by every Kiowa at Anadarko . . . except on allotment day. Then some of them have use for me . . . until my food has been eaten. When it is time to eat their food, there is not enough. They throw rocks at me to run me off. And when I come back, they beat me with sticks. And yet . . . I am not a Methodist, I am a Kiowa. I do not think they are true Kiowas."

"They are Kiowas." Daha-hen turned from the boy. "Kiowas like to stay alive. They leave their babies and old people when they are inconvenient. A woman will leave her blind husband when he cannot provide. A warrior expects to be left when he cannot keep up, when he holds the others back."

"You may leave me then, when I cannot keep up," said Thomas.

"I have never left a man I took to ride with me," Daha-hen said softly as he remounted. "I have no need of you, Thomas Young Man."

Thomas sat quietly. "It is said around the fires, when the old men talk, that you always rode with only one or two men on raids. One of those men, like Quitan, was usually a Mexican who spoke Spanish."

"Quitan was a warrior, not a *dapom*," said Daha-hen.

"But he was once a *dapom*. You made him a warrior. And when he was at your side, you had great confidence in your dealings with the Mexicans and Comancheros. Is that not so?"

Daha-hen looked at the ragged, earnest boy and wondered why he listened, why he bothered with an answer. "It is so."

"Well," said Thomas Young Man, "I both speak and read English. I am a great asset to you where you are going."

Daha-hen turned his horse back toward Elk Creek. "You may ride along while I think on this, Thomas Young Man," he said. "But it may be a long ride for nothing. Your horse may not be able to keep up. You are probably too young and inexperienced. I have already several young men to help me." Daha-hen nudged his pony forward. The boy mounted his scrawny pony and put him to a trot. "I never rode with your father, Thomas Young Man. I did not like him."

"I myself never knew him, Daha-hen," Thomas said. "But many times I have thought very little of him for leaving my mother and myself alone."

"He did not leave you exactly by choice," said Daha-hen. "I heard he was killed going upstream against Bad Hand's troops in Palo Duro Cañon. His actions gave others time to escape."

"We did not escape," the boy reflected. "They kept us in the stone corral at Fort Sill. There was little food or shelter. We only had a buffalo robe. Some had nothing. The women and children with strong men had a better chance. It was very hard for us. My mother was all I had. She was not bad then."

The firing upstream sounded like popcorn exploding from the fire. Daha-hen rested and ate from the abandoned cooking pot as he watched the panic around him. Young men had been running, catching their ponies, painting their faces. They were young enough to be afraid they would miss the fighting. But Daha-hen had known they would not. This time there were many soldiers, sliding and slipping down the southern trail into the cañon. This time there would be enough fighting, even for the young men.

Daha-hen had taken more food. He had time. The fighting was still in the upper villages. The People were in a panic, trying to find out what was happening, but Daha-hen knew. Two days before he had seen the white tents of the troops. Like many of the experienced men he had been going about the country. He had tracked the troops in the moonlight. He had fired on them at a watering hole.

Yesterday, on foot, he had risen from the tall grass, killed an eks-a-pana, a soldier, and scalped him before he hit the ground. He had wanted the big sorrel horse the man rode. But the horse had turned out to be of no use to Daha-hen. It was wounded in the ankle, shot by the soldier as he had fired down at the Indian. He had left it. Looking back, Daha-hen saw Black Horse leading the sorrel away. That Quohadi would take anything. It would, of course, be a good enough horse with time to heal. But Daha-hen knew that there would not be time. Time had run out for the People.

Time had been running out a long time now — since Satanta and Big Tree had been sent to the Texas prison. Now the People were ending. Soon all the fighting would be over. The young men were right, after all, in rushing to the sound of the guns.

"You, there," Chief K'ya-been, Red War Bonnet, called out to Daha-hen, not recognizing his back. "Get your horse and go see what is wrong with those women who are crying. Get them up into the side cañon where the climbing is easier."

Daha-hen turned, revealing his painted face to Red War Bonnet. Black eyes looked out from the black paint that hid the upper portion of his face. Daha-hen wiped his hands on a discarded cloth. "The world is truly changing. Do you give orders to me now, Red War Bonnet?"

The chief winced, knowing the insult he had made to the great warrior. Red War Bonnet's face was painted, and he was wearing his buffalo-horn cap. He was leaving for the battle. Yet, as chief of the band, he had had to see to all of his people. "I will find someone else, Daha-

62

hen," he said. "A young inexperienced man can do this thing."

"Go on, Red War Bonnet," Daha-hen said, licking the final bits of food from his back teeth. "I will see to this thing."

Red War Bonnet did not wait. He whirled the horse, looking about him for the young men and warriors who would follow him to the fight. He hesitated a moment. The women and children were running away, back from the fighting. They were climbing the steep walls of the cañon. The children were crying. An old woman had fallen. Her daughter and granddaughter were trying to lift her up, as the horses and riders danced about them.

Red War Bonnet whirled again. "Ahe!" he shouted, and rode away. The young men followed.

Daha-hen watched them go, breathed the dust of their departure. The energy was gone with the men. There were no more shouts to arms, no war songs, no horses whinnying, no eager hoofs tapping the ground.

Daha-hen looked about the tumbled village. A young warrior dashed to catch the others. Cooking pots were turned over. Hide frames and drying racks lay broken. Only a few women struggled to roll up the teepee covers and nest them in the fork of the poles. They knew the white men burned lodges. But it was not so easy to set them on fire when the covers were not on the ground. Some might survive.

He heard the women then. Most made no sound, but moved swiftly up the cañon. They were making their way toward the rim, leaving the false safety of the camp. Only a few carried robes and blankets.

You will need robes and blankets and food, Daha-hen thought to himself. Your men cannot stop so many sol-

63

diers. And these soldiers will burn everything before they leave. If you can come back, there will be nothing.

He heard the wailing, then, the anguish that had caused Red War Bonnet to call out to him. Daha-hen slipped onto his pony and followed the sound.

There were three women. One, with a baby in a cradleboard on her back, was half crazed, slapping at the hands of the other two women as they attempted to lead her or take the cradle from her back.

"Give me the baby," Daha-hen said from above them. "Then you can go faster. I will help you."

"No!" the woman screamed, trying to twist herself free of the grasp of the two women. "No. Let us throw it away! Yes, throw it away!"

"I had rather throw you away," Daha-hen said. "Here," he rode closer and reached down, "here. Hand me that baby. Do it now." Yellow Walking Woman looked up into his face. Daha-hen took the baby from the two women as they lifted the cradleboard from her back and fastened it to his saddle. Then the warrior bent, wrapped his hand and forearm around the woman's arm, and swung her up behind him. "Now you can get away faster. I will help you."

With the baby before him and the woman behind him, Daha-hen rode back into the village. The woman beat her fists against his back. "No, no," she shouted at the warrior.

He reached back and held her to him with his free hand. "Be quiet and hold on," Daha-hen said as he let go of her and ran the pony into the village. Swiftly he bent from the saddle and snatched a buffalo robe from the ground. He threw it over the baby and turned the little horse. Another swoop and he had a bag of dried meat.

Laying into the little horse, he raced for the cañon.

In the small side cañon the women and children were climbing. Some were already near the top. The women who had been with Yellow Walking Woman were there. Daha-hen pulled the horse to a stop. He tossed the bag of meat to one woman and the buffalo robe to the other. Twisting and with one arm he caught Yellow Walking Woman's waist and eased her down to the ground. He handed the baby in the cradleboard to her.

"Take this child and climb. The climb is not steep here. You can make it with the baby. These women will help you. You will need the food and blanket. Do not leave them." He said this to Yellow Walking Woman, but his eyes looked at the other women. "Do not leave them."

He watched as Yellow Walking Woman — beautiful Yellow Walking Woman, long black hair falling over her shoulders — received the child onto her back and began to climb. She never looked back. The other women followed. Yellow Walking Woman had not even known him who loved her so much.

This Thomas Young Man was the baby of Yellow Walking Woman and Young Man. Daha-hen had saved his life at Palo Duro, not from the white soldiers but from his own mother. Now she had left him once again. So Daha-hen must help him grow up.

Chapter Seven

"Love lifted me . . . love lifted me. When nothing else could help, love l-i-i-i-f-ted me," sang Thomas Young Man.

Daha-hen jerked at the unnatural noise. Slowly he turned in the saddle and observed the boy with head thrown back, singing in the prairie heat. "Do not sing," said Daha-hen.

"I am stirring myself up," said Thomas.

"You are warning every living thing that someone passes." Daha-hen turned back.

"Do not all warriors sing?"

"They sing, but to themselves," said Daha-hen. "They sing a different song. Going away, going away . . . going away, maybe I will die. Still I am going away."

"Not very cheerful," said Thomas. "Is that your song?"

"I do not sing or pray for power." Daha-hen rode without turning around.

"Why not?"

Daha-hen kept riding. He did not answer the boy's question.

"Why not?"

"I am thinking how to tell you," said Daha-hen. He kept riding.

"Yes," the boy prompted. "I am listening. The others

say you are peculiar. Is it because you do not sing or pray?"

"I do not sing or pray because I am a man. There is power enough in that. A bundle of feathers that men can carry about or a stuffed owl cannot protect me or tell me what I will do. Only I can determine what I do." Daha-hen had found the words at last.

"That is peculiar."

"It is not peculiar," replied Daha-hen. "It is so."

"Still, it would be comforting to have the support of a greater force than one's self," Thomas Young Man spoke his thoughts.

"It is comforting to know your own strength and depend on it."

"What if you were without strength?"

"I am never without strength."

"But what if you were wounded?" Thomas persisted.

"I have been wounded. I counted on myself."

"But what if you were so badly wounded, you could not count on yourself?" Thomas would not let go of the thought.

"Then I would die," stated Daha-hen.

"Are you not afraid to die?"

"No." The warrior anticipated the next question. "Do not say why, Thomas Young Man. It is because, if death is a good country, I will be satisfied because I have been a man while I lived. If there is no land after this, I will not know it or care when I am dead. Now be quiet. You are just a boy, following along."

The pair rode single file across the rolling plains back toward Elk Creek and the beginning of their journey. At noon the sun stood over them, sucking the very shadows away. Thomas Young Man drooped on his pony.

At times he lay forward over the saddle horn, resting his cheek against the coarse mane of the horse. Daha-hen never looked around to see if he were still following.

Long past noon they came to the first water they had seen in several hours. Thomas sighed at the sight. His pony was eager for a drink, but the boy restrained him.

"Guess we cannot just canter on up to the water and shade?" he said aloud.

"We will get there, Thomas Young Man. We will drink deep and rest our ponies. And while we are going there, we will have time to look about for any danger."

"Do you expect danger, Daha-hen?" the boy asked. "There is no danger any more. The wars are over."

"I always expect the unexpected," answered Daha-hen. "And I am alive still after many battles and many years."

In the shade of the pecan trees man and boy slid to the ground and let the horses drink. Daha-hen cupped his hand and lifted water to his mouth. He watched young Thomas kneel beside the stream, cup water in his hand, and lift it while his eyes looked at the other shore.

"Tell me, Thomas Young Man, why do you drink like a warrior when you do not expect danger?" asked Daha-hen, settling back against the fallen log.

The boy smiled slightly. "The Methodists."

Daha-hen studied the boy and waited for the ever-flowing fountain of his mouth to fill the silence.

"The Methodists tell a story of Old Gideon. They always say 'Old Gideon.' Old Gideon found favor with God and man. He started out against the enemy with a lot of men, thousands. But there were too many for God to do a miracle. I mean, it would look like just a regular fight if his bunch of men beat the other bunch of men.

So God told Old Gideon to send home those who wanted to go. A lot of them left. There were still too many. Finally God said to Old Gideon: 'Take the men down to the stream to get a drink. The ones that kneel and drink with their faces in the water, send them home. The ones that bring water to their faces and drink from their hands, take them with you.' There weren't many of them. Just enough for the miracle. I always wanted to pass the test, so I could go along and see a miracle. So I practiced drinking that way in case I ever needed it."

Daha-hen wiped the thin wet mustaches at the corners of his mouth with both hands. "In your ignorance you have passed the test, Thomas. Without a warrior's education you have done a warrior's act. If you had guzzled like a horse, I'd have sent you home."

Thomas smiled and lay back against the log beside Daha-hen. The warrior handed the boy a strip of dried beef. "Did Old Gideon have food, boy, or was that another miracle?" The boy hesitated. "Go on take it. Starvin' ain't no good." Daha-hen spoke the last words in English.

Thomas Young Man sat up. "You speak English!"

"Sometimes I speak a little English," said Daha-hen, this time in Kiowa. "Satanta spoke five languages. I only know two well, Kiowa and Comanche, because I lived with both of them. I have pretty good pieces of Mexican and Cheyenne. Over time it's gotten kind of mixed together. Most of the time I don't know which I'm using. But I don't have much English, mostly cuss words and cries, like, 'Stop!,' 'Don't shoot!,' 'Where's your paper?' I always have it in my hand because I don't know how to say where else it is."

"How come you lived with the Comanches?"

"Oh, there was the time of my disgrace. I was prickly

69

as a cactus and couldn't be around people. So I went into the no-water country." Daha-hen's words came slowly as he set the dried meat in his cheek to soften.

"Like Moses," the boy interjected.

"I don't know Moses." Daha-hen exaggerated the word Moses. "You know more Methodists than Kiowas, Thomas Young Man. Let's get going."

"Tell me about going to be with the Comanches."

"Not much to tell," Daha-hen continued. "I went into the no-water country. . . ."

Daha-hen told the story to the boy, Thomas Young Man, but the picture of another young man arose in his mind.

Zepko-eet-te had passed through the no-water country without seeing it. His shame had wrapped him in a fog that prevented his notice of anything outside his own pain. He could think of nothing but his shame and foolishness, the mark on his life. He had played the thoughts about Yellow Walking Woman and Young Man from every side. He had seen Young Man standing before his lodge, ridiculing him, throwing aside the door covering and revealing Yellow Walking Woman, with the women attending her frozen feet. He had heard Yellow Walking Woman say again that she herself had chosen Young Man, a better man than he was. Zepko-eet-te always found himself guilty and disgraced. In that time, his heart was on the ground.

His father's training had led him and guided him even when his own thoughts were far away. He had found water. He had hunted when game came near. His cooking was more habit than hunger. He could not say what he ate or if he ate. He had slept fretfully or not at all. When

70

exhaustion had caught him at last, he had slept in the sand, in thickets, or under rocky ledges. The horse, his only companion, had grazed and watched.

Zepko-eet-te did not blame his father. Big Bow loved him, and that love was too great for the boy ever to think that his father would betray him or try to make a fool of him. No, he had betrayed himself in his blindness over the woman. Big Bow had come to stand with him against Young Man. He had remained silent and let Zepko-eet-te direct him, a renowned warrior, against Young Man. No, his father was not to blame. He had warned him to stay away. He had given him time to think in his lodge that long night, time to see the woman's fickleness. Big Bow could not have known Young Man would come home and find her with her feet nearly frozen, waiting for the young warrior. He could not have known that Zepko-eet-te, who had been held high, would be held up to ridicule.

Still, the boy hurt. At first, he thought he had hurt because Yellow Walking Woman was not with him. He had thought of her by his side, in his arms, beside his fire, cooking for them. And, then, he had thought about the girl's words. She had chosen Young Man herself.

She was a liar, drawing Zepko-eet-te into what he had thought was her despair, making him her champion against her husband, dancing him about with her words and soft glances. But in the end her husband had stood her protector against the young usurper who would humble him by taking his wife.

She had played both men cleverly, he thought, securing her place with one, destroying the other. She, his beloved, had found another man to be his superior. He could not even go back and kill Young Man and take the woman because she had spoken before all the People that she

71

did not want him. Yellow Walking Woman had left him nothing — no illusion and no recourse.

Somewhere in the desert Zepko-eet-te had realized that he could have killed her husband or been killed himself for the fickleness of Yellow Walking Woman. She, in her treachery, could not have lost. Either way, she would have been the beautiful creature that men were willing to kill and die for. Zepko-eet-te saw the treachery, the vanity, as clearly as he had seen the beauty and noble cause. He put the woman aside. In fact, the young man put aside all women, for all women were Yellow Walking Woman to him. The taste of her was bitter in his mouth.

Still Zepko-eet-te could not put aside his shame. The ridicule of Young Man and the laughter of the people had rung in his ears on the ever-blowing wind. The shame had gone deeply into his heart. In his mind the boy felt that his life was tarnished, irreparably blotted.

Looking at his haggard face, his dirty hands and clothes in the reflection from the stream, Zepko-eet-te had seen himself a dapom. These filthy ones, lowest of the classes of Kiowa society, were outright bad characters, misfits, and no accounts well beyond shame and redemption. This dapom gazing back from the water was what he — Zepko-eet-te, the son of chiefs — had become.

His father and his grandfather were men of high rank, onde. All his skill and daring were to attain for himself what they had held before him. He grieved for his place beside them. He bathed and dressed his hair. He gazed back into the water. He did not look a dapom any more. Still, he was ruined, worthless. He must find a way to show that he was still strong, still worthy of his father and grandfather.

He rode away from the little watercourse thinking —

if he did not die of his broken heart and disgrace, he must live and show himself to be strong.

The horse trembled beneath Zepko-eet-te's knees, and the young man looked up from his reverie. Below him men were fighting — Comanches and Mexican lancers. He saw a rope fly through the air, circle a young Indian's neck. His arm and shoulder struggled up in the loop to keep the noose from strangling him.

Zepko-eet-te did not think, did not hesitate. He plunged his pony off the ridge and down into the dusty field of battle. Riding among the Comanches and lancers, he grabbed a lance stuck into the ground and rode hard after the rider dragging the young Indian. Zepko-eet-te set the long weapon in his arm as he pursued. He pounded on, focused on the red coat of the soldier. The soldier turned to see his prisoner, to enjoy the pain he inflicted. When he saw Zepko-eet-te closing in, he dropped the rope. He dug heavy spurs into his horse's heaving sides. Just as he turned to bring his weapon up against Zepko-eet-te, the long steel blade of the young warrior's lance caught him in the chest. The Kiowa's charging pony drove the point through him. He fell backward, pinned where he lay.

Zepko-eet-te spun the pony, brought it to the squirming soldier. He dropped quickly to the ground, caught the lancer's hair in his fist, pulled his head against his chest, and cut the scalp away smoothly from front to back. Standing up, he dropped the dead man back against the earth. The fight around him still continued. Men and horses screamed and churned the dry earth.

Zepko-eet-te jumped onto the standing pony's back and rode toward the Comanche who had been dragged behind

73

the lancer. Bloody and dirty, without weapons, he was just rising to his knees. Zepko-eet-te whooped and rode toward him. With one arm he reached down, caught the man, and pulled him onto the running horse. Together they rode for the timbered stream.

Among the trees the young men drew up to breathe and consider the action. The lancers' dust rose behind them, blurring the red of their jackets as they rode away. Some of the Comanches rode after them, mocking them with feeble pursuit as a man stamps his foot at a cowed dog.

Zepko-eet-te breathed deeply and looked around him. The trees were green and moving in the breeze that cooled his sweating body. He felt the horse's sides, heard the blowing breath. His hand felt the damp coarse hair as he patted the animal's shoulder. The earth was bright and clear beyond the shade where he sat. Sunlight danced among the tree shadows and on the water. Dust rose as the other Comanches rode toward them. The world was there again. Zepko-eet-te's grief had passed.

The Comanche men circled around Zepko-eet-te. "You are a great warrior," the toyapke said. "You have saved my father's favorite son with your daring."

Zepko-eet-te signed that he did not understand. The Comanche spoke again in the sign language the Plains peoples shared. "I could not have gone home and told our father his son was killed, so you have saved me from becoming a wanderer. Accept my hand in friendship." The large man put out his hand and arm, and Zepko-eet-te took it. "You will always have a place beside my fire. What is your name, young man?"

"I am Zepko-eet-te, son of Big Bow, son of Big Bow," he said.

The Comanche, whose name was Fire Rising Up, pointed at the medicine bag that hung about Zepko-eet-te's neck and made the sign for powerful. "You have great medicine," he said. "I would have such medicine for my son."

Zepko-eet-te's hand came to the bag. He had forgotten it was there. He suddenly remembered the words he had heard when he became toyapke. "This is your medicine . . . to step out without trinkets or images men carry about. Be strong in yourself. I have made you complete. Your courage will draw my power." He now grasped it, broke the thong that held it, and handed it to Fire Rising Up. "I give this to your son."

Chapter Eight

"So I gave Fire Rising Up the medicine bag," Daha-hen told Thomas Young Man. "It was just a bag of teeth and bones. A man must have medicine inside. He must believe in himself and live in that belief, not in such things. And that was how a Kiowa came to ride with the Comanches and learn their language. Together I rode with them through Mexico, taking horses, taking scalps. They taught me the land and their ways. I often rested beside the Quohadi fires. In every battle I rode without medicine. And in every battle, I prevailed. That is how I became Daha-hen, Man Without Medicine."

Daha-hen stood up, dusted the debris from his white man's pants, and gathered his reins. He looked at Thomas Young Man who stood mesmerized by the tale. He finished the story quickly.

"The Quohadi did not make too much of that name for they are not religious, but practical. They have little use for owl prophets. But it has worried the Kiowas a great deal. They have never trusted me."

Thomas Young Man walked to his scrawny pony without a word. Daha-hen watched him swing himself up, turn the animal, and start away. The boy caught himself and stopped. "Where are we going, Man Without Medicine?"

"I am going back to my lodge," Daha-hen said, shaking

his head. "Surely you have heard coup stories before, Thomas Young Man."

The boy shook his head. "The men at the agency do not talk much. Mostly I am run away from their food and fires. I have to beg to hear anything from my older brother or uncle. They are looking at farming. The Methodists have good stories, though."

"You know that I once knew another man named Thomas. He was with the Quakers. We did not like each other. He was a friend of Kicking Bird's. He came from the Wichita Agency and lived with Kicking Bird's people. I was not for peace as Kicking Bird was. I wanted to fight white men and drive them back. There are things you cannot drive back. You cannot drive back the night or the day, when their time has come, or a child when it will be born. I was wrong, but I had to see if they could be driven back. A man must see what can be done." Daha-hen paused, then added: "I have decided to call you Thomassey."

Thomas followed Daha-hen across the prairie and into the growing darkness. He rode silently for many miles. "Kicking Bird was killed by medicine," he said.

"Some people say that he was killed by Mamanti's medicine," Daha-hen said. "Maybe he just died. Or maybe somebody helped him die. Mamanti was an owl prophet. They always have tricks. You never know what they are doing behind your back. They always want something for their doings.

"When we were going on raids and we stopped to rest, that owl prophet blew up his little owl skin and made owl sounds. All the men went to see him to learn how they would do in the fighting. They had to pay him little things, sometimes even a horse, to see if they would have a victory or die."

"How could he make the owl talk?" asked Thomas.

"He could not make the owl talk," said Daha-hen. "He just had an owl skin. He blew it up. Made owl sounds. Then he told the men, for a price, what the owl said."

"How did he know what the owl said?"

"There was no owl, Thomassey, just Mamanti. He made up the owl, and he made up the prophecies to get the gifts the men gave him." Daha-hen rode on. He continued: "Well, once he had a real owl, a little burrowing owl from a prairie dog tunnel. He brought it out. It hooted. The men came to hear their fortunes, and they paid Mamanti. That was pretty good until Hau-va-te came up and had no money to pay. He did not want to have a bad prophecy, so he killed the owl on Mamanti's arm. He said it should have known he had a stick in his hand if it was a prophet. Most of the men turned back on that raid. I never liked to ride with a large group of men. I never liked to ride with an owl prophet."

"The People are afraid of the old *tai-bo*. They say he is a sorcerer," the boy remarked. "He can cough up feathers."

"The People were afraid of Satank most of all. Have you heard from your people of that old man?" asked Daha-hen.

"No."

"Satank was a Real Dog, *Koitsenko*, and a Yellow Shield. Those warriors would stake themselves to the ground by driving a lance or arrow through a sash tied around them. They would fight where they stood until they were killed or until someone came and got them loose. Satanta hated that. He said it was stupid for a man with a good horse to fight on foot. But Satank was an old-time warrior. And the People had great respect for him . . . maybe it was just fear. He was a scary old man.

"When his favorite son was killed, he went to Mexico and killed and scalped two men and brought the bones home on his son's horse. He had his son's bones kept on a bed in the boy's lodge. He had feasts for him there. Satank's women moved that lodge and set it up again whenever the camp moved. Skinny old Satank led the bones on a horse everywhere he went."

"He led a bag of bones around with him?" asked Thomas.

"They were wrapped in a red flannel blanket and a blue flannel blanket. And old Satank led his son around with him, not bones. That was what was scary," said Daha-hen.

"Could Satank cough up feathers?"

"He coughed up a knife once. When they were taking him to prison."

"In Florida?" asked the boy.

"It is very hard to finish a sentence with you, Thomassey. The soldiers were taking him to prison in Texas. That was maybe three or four years before the chiefs were sent to Florida. You were not yet born. We had had a big raid. We were tired of the white men. Nothing had changed since the Medicine Lodge treaty. The buffalo hunters were coming south. The Texans were stealing our horses. The surveyors were out on our land. So we went on a raid. A young man named Gunshot was killed in that raid. We killed seven freighters. Some others got away and went to Fort Richardson. The big general, Sherman, was there. He was very angry. After that he would not rest on us.

79

"I will tell you this, Thomassey. Gunshot was a foolish young man. He could not hold himself back. He rode ahead of everyone to count first coup. When he hit the wagon, one of the teamsters raised the tarp and shot him in the face. His jaw was blown away, and we could see the inside of his mouth through the blood. We knew that he was dead right then. But Gunshot lived for several days and got his own vengeance against the man who shot him. The Kiowas took that man out of his wagon and tied him on a wagon wheel and built a fire under his head. Gunshot got to see all of this. He also cut out the man's tongue when his hollering became a nuisance. I think Gunshot was greatly to blame for the general's attitude. His greed started everything off wrong. He had no discipline."

"Cut out the man's tongue?" asked Thomas.

"He was very loud," answered Daha-hen. "Do not Methodists sometimes act harshly?"

"Well, there was lots of fighting in the old times of the Hebrew children," said Thomas Young Man. "Little David once cut off the foreskins of two-hundred Philistines so he could marry King Saul's daughter, Michal."

Daha-hen twisted in his saddle and looked at young Thomas. "Two hundred?"

The boy nodded.

Daha-hen turned back in his saddle and rode thoughtfully. "That is not as useful as horses for a marriage gift."

Chapter Nine

When Daha-hen reached his home, he slid slowly from the horse and stretched his back. Many Tongues came out to him and looked closely to see how he was. The children were about his legs, holding him, wanting to be lifted.

"You got the paper?" Many Tongues asked.

Daha-hen reached into his shirt and held the paper for her to see. He smiled at her and led the children by their heads into the brush arbor.

"Who is that *dapom?*" asked Elk.

Daha-hen turned and saw Thomas Young Man still sitting on his shaggy pony. He looked then at his nephew, strong and sure, confident of his place among his family and the People. Something in Elk's words irritated Daha-hen. "Get down and come inside to eat, Thomassey," said Daha-hen.

Slowly the tattered boy dropped down and came toward the family.

"I know this one, Uncle," said Elk. "He is worthless, a joke to the People. His mother was killed by a drunken soldier at Fort Sill. His brother and uncle have thrown him away. He is nothing."

"He is a guest here, Elk," said Daha-hen. "The Kiowas remember hospitality even when they host their worst enemies. We do not make trouble where our women and

81

children are. Go inside and leave this boy alone."

Elk shrugged and went into the arbor. "He is no more a guest than a camp dog," he muttered beyond Daha-hen's hearing.

Many Tongues brought out the tin plates she had gotten from the trading store and filled them with boiled meat. She had made a sweet cornbread and laid it beside the meat. She poured coffee into mugs for her husband and nephew and the guest. Looking at Thomas, she added a small extra to each of his servings.

As the men ate, Many Tongues took the little boys to bed inside the teepee. They giggled and laughed and popped up as she tried to cover them.

"You may listen quietly," she said. "Lie here where you can see."

"That boy is funny looking," Buckskin, the older boy, said.

Many Tongues placed her fingers over his lips. "He is our guest." She lay down beside the children and looked back toward the fire.

"Funny looking," she heard the younger boy say softly. Then there were giggles as the children snuggled down to watch the adults and hear their words.

"Broken Stick and Gnat Catcher will go with us after the thieves," said Elk. "They have good horses." Daha-hen saw the look his nephew threw at Thomas Young Man. "We can find these thieves and get back our horses."

Daha-hen continued to eat as the other young men rode up. Loud Talker's son, Broken Stick, did have a good horse, but Daha-hen did not think it could run buffalo. The boy had not trained it properly. Loud Talker never had good buffalo ponies.

"Get down, Kiowas. Come and eat," said Daha-hen. The youths entered and sat across the fire beside Elk. "Who lost horses?" asked Daha-hen.

"Everyone along the creek lost horses," said Elk.

"Does anyone else want to ride after the horse thieves?" The young men dropped their heads. Daha-hen smiled. "We do not need a large war party for this. Young men are sometimes best on a raid. It is a way to make a place for yourself."

Thomas looked up from his eating.

"Tell us, Uncle, how you became a *toyapke* when you were our age." Elk spoke proudly for he knew his uncle was exceptional. Few men became chiefs when so young.

Daha-hen washed the grease from his fingers in the water Many Tongues had left for them. He wiped his hands dry. "I was a young man of seventeen summers. I had been on many raids with my father as a camp boy. I had been on one raid as a warrior beside my father.

"A pipe bearer came to us. It was winter then, not the time for raiding. But the *toyapke* had seen the Navajo herds in the fall and knew they had many ponies. He also knew that they would not expect a raid in winter. I was eager to go. My father already had many horses to care for, and he did not want to go. But my uncle, White Wolf, my mother's brother, knew I wanted to go, so he agreed to go. . . ."

White Wolf tossed a piece of bark into the current. He watched the bark whirl away, past the Pecos ford. With narrowed eyes, he looked upstream. Recrossing the rising river in winter could be trouble. He said nothing, but waited for Catches Hold, the toyapke, *leader, pipe bearer,*

83

of the raiding party to make his decision.

"The two youngest boys will stay here with our horses and supplies," Catches Hold said. "We will take only one mule, cross the river, and move down upon the Navajo herds before they know we are in their country. Be cheerful, my friends, in a few days our long ride and walk will bring us each many horses."

Zepko-eet-te smiled to himself at the thought of returning with many horses. His father was a famous horsetaker. He would be like him. His own medicine was good. He carried worthy weapons. The horse his father gave him was generous and strong. His skills with weapon and horse, with the land and with men, were ready to be tested and proved.

Many times before Zepko-eet-te had gone out as horsekeeper and cook like the young boys with this party. Since childhood he had learned the lessons of the land and seasons. His whole life had brought him to this moment of crossing. A chill ran over him. Was he worthy of his father and grandfather? His heart pounded, eager to rush across the Pecos and discover the answer.

A slap on his shoulder recalled him from his reverie. "We cross," White Wolf, his mother's brother, said. The tall copper warrior pointed ahead with his bow.

Lifting his rolled blanket, arrow, and quivers, Zepko-eet-te stepped quickly into the waist-deep water ahead of White Wolf. No sound escaped him as the freezing water engulfed his lower body. For a moment he wondered why they must walk into the enemy's country when they had such good horses. The cold air stung him as he walked out of the water on the far side of the ford. But, as he walked along behind the others, the chill passed, and he gradually became dry again.

84

The Kiowa raiders walked throughout the winter day across the flat miles of sand that the wind pushed into swirling dunes. Occasionally, White Wolf looked back over his shoulder. At first Zepko-eet-te thought he was checking him. But his father's friend, his mother's brother, would not embarrass him by showing obvious concern for his ability to keep up.

Catches Hold called a brief halt. The men sat down to rest. A boulder provided Zepko-eet-te a firm back support as he relaxed his hands upon his knees. He was careful to watch and listen to the mature warriors about him. If they ate, he, too, would draw forth a piece of jerked meat from the small pouch he wore. If they did not, he could go for many more hours without eating. He looked back at the young boys who led the mule. He frowned. The smiles faded from their lips, and they became quiet. Their deference to him made him feel good, wise. They knew he had brought back a captive already. He turned back to the older men. White Wolf chewed a sliver of jerked meat slowly, letting the juices of his mouth soften the tough dry strip. Zepko-eet-te, too, ate.

A little rest and the signal passed to move out. White Wolf picked up his shield and his muzzle-loading rifle. He moved very slowly, waiting, letting the others, even the boys with the mule, move out ahead of him. He signed for Zepko-eet-te to precede him. And the young warrior walked on. Zepko-eet-te watched the men ahead of him and wondered why White Wolf hung back.

Zepko-eet-te was trained to observe and think like a chief — to see things, relations other men might miss. His mind considered the party's situation. They were well equipped but afoot in their enemy's land. Catches Hold, the leader, was eager for horses, sure of horses. He had led good raids before against the Navajos. The men wanted to share his success. The men liked Catches Hold and his promise of horses. He walked proudly before them, carrying the pipe stem upward, according to his place and the People's custom.

But White Wolf, a brave and famous warrior, stayed back. Was he losing his eagerness for danger? Zepko-eet-te threw that thought away quickly. No man among the raiders was at his prime like White Wolf. Everything about him spoke of his success and his power. He would be first into the danger if he led the raiders. And, then, Zepko-eet-te knew. The danger that concerned White Wolf most was not in front, but from behind. With each step they traveled deeper into Navajo country. They had left no rear guard. Anyone who crossed their trail could follow and attack without warning. Zepko-eet-te drew in his breath. As the trek continued farther into the land, he occasionally glanced over his shoulder on a turn or a high place. Sometimes he caught White Wolf standing a long moment, watching the farthest horizon from which they had come.

At nightfall Catches Hold brought the small party into camp beneath an overhang within a cañon. It gave good protection from the variable weather. Back down the cañon there was good grazing for the mule that carried their camp gear. One of the boys, Bird-Seen-In-Winter, took the mule back to the grass while the other boy prepared the small supper the warriors consumed. Zepko-eet-te ate quietly with his shield, bow, and quiver at his side.

The weapons were still new to him — treasures of his first manhood. Always a warrior of the People must keep his weapons close. Zepko-eet-te saw a man once, an outcast, a man of shame to himself and to the People. He had thrown down his weapons and had run away to safety, having left the women and children and old ones. Many people had died because of his cowardice at the place called Scratching Rock. Their enemies, the Osages, had surprised them and had killed them as they had tried to climb the rocks, to find shelter even in the holes of the earth. Their enemies had put their heads in brass kettles. It was a great sadness. The coward who had deserted them would never know peace or acceptance again.

Kiowa boys learned quickly what was expected of a man. A warrior always engaged and drew the enemy away from the women and children. His was the arm of protection that kept the most vulnerable safe. The bravest warriors, like Old Elk who had died in the summer, sometimes tied a sash around themselves and pinned the loose end to the earth with arrow or lance. Self-staked, they stood and fought until released by a comrade or by death. They did not run. Zepko-eet-te knew a hundred tales of valor. He knew the men who stood like his father and his grandfather. He knew he must stand with them or lose his place among the People. No question of choice ever entered his mind. Zepko-eet-te was a son of the People.

"By afternoon we will see the Navajo herds," Catches Hold directed them. "By nightfall tomorrow we will have our own herd and head for home. Sleep well. Be ready."

After supper and a little talk the men rolled themselves one by one into their blankets and slept the good sleep of tired men, the restorative, renewing sleep of men with a mission. White Wolf sat a long time after the others slept, then lay down at the far edge of the overhang near

Zepko-eet-te. From there he could see an attack coming from the valley below, and from there he could escape being trapped in the overhang. Zepko-eet-te felt pleased with himself. He had chosen his resting place wisely.

Before he slept, the young man thought of the day's journey. He remembered each landmark of the terrain. He listened to the camp boys' giggle for a few minutes. They soon became silent. Zepko-eet-te thought of the test before him. He felt a prickly sensation on the surface of his skin. Something was coming. Be ready. And then, just before he fell asleep, he tasted the cold night air with all his senses. It was good to be young, to contemplate bravery and honor, to live free, to be about a man's work, a man's destiny. This was a great time in his life. Zepko-eet-te fell softly to sleep.

No sentinel watched over the sleeping camp. None had been posted.

The Navajos had cut Catches Hold's and the horsetakers' trail before sunset. They knew a Kiowa raiding party had come to take what was theirs unless they could keep it. Reality was simple among the Indians. What you possessed was yours only if you could keep it. The Navajos intended for their enemies to take nothing and to leave their lives in the cañon. Silently, in the darkness, they moved up the long, ascending cañon and hid themselves among the rocks to wait for morning.

Chapter Ten

Zepko-eet-te woke early before light came to the cañon floor. He lay still a few minutes, listening, waking up, and then he sat up. Standing, pulling the blanket over his shoulder, he walked to the sleeping boys and pushed them awake with his foot.

"Go up the side cañon and bring fresh water," he said.

The boys rubbed themselves awake and gathered the buffalo paunches to carry water in. Zepko-eet-te watched the sleepy boys walk away. Not long ago he was a sleepy boy, bringing water for the men. He turned and went down the cañon to get the mule. As he approached the animal, he watched it grazing. Suddenly the mule's head came up, nose lifted into the wind blowing against Zepko-eet-te. The mule whickered and backed against the rope that held him. He planted his hind quarters and jumped to one side. Zepko-eet-te saw a shadow dart between some rocks. He stepped back into the darkness and listened and waited. The mule was wary, not frantic as it would have been if it had caught the scent of a mountain cat or bear. Zepko-eet-te saw a second shadow move. He turned immediately in the darkness where he waited and ran quietly back to camp.

Moving from man to man, Zepko-eet-te whispered, "Be awake. Wake up. The enemy is near. Wake up. Get ready. Be awake."

As Zepko-eet-te moved among the men, the boys ran back into camp. A burst of gunfire followed them. Kneeling beside White Wolf, Zepko-eet-te saw the explosive fire against the darkness. White Wolf was already awake and had his rifle and necessities. Other warriors brushed past Zepko-eet-te. Snatching their weapons, they scattered towards the sides of the cañon. The camp was a fixed target for the shooters out in the darkness. There was cover along the cañon.

"Run," said Catches Hold as he went by. "Get out of this death place."

"Come," said White Wolf. "There is good cover in the cottonwoods."

Zepko-eet-te and the boys, Bird-Seen-In-Winter and Finds-A-Coyote-Pup, followed him. Once hidden, they tried to discover the location and number of their unseen enemy.

"How many?" asked Zepko-eet-te.

"Too many," said White Wolf. The flashes of the discharges showed the Navajos' advance as the Kiowas retreated up the cañon. They moved slowly, expecting defenders in the camp. White Wolf and Zepko-eet-te watched silently. The first Navajo stepped into the camp site. No defender confronted him. Quickly another and another Navajo came into the abandoned camp. The growing daylight revealed the emptiness of the overhang, the abandoned food and blankets. One of the Navajos kicked through the crumpled blankets.

White Wolf raised his long rifle, braced it against the tree that concealed him. Zepko-eet-te and the boys followed his preparation. Their eyes recorded every movement the esteemed warrior made. Trying to see the target, Zepko-eet-te glanced quickly at the men pillaging the camp. But White Wolf's swift movement followed by rigid stillness drew him back. He watched the squinting eye, the strong finger joint wrapped over the trigger. Silent years passed. Sound exploded in fire out of the muzzle, hit the smooth rock wall, and crashed back upon them. Zepko-eet-te's eyes slammed shut and open. His ears ached. One of the Navajo men fell. White Wolf grunted in satisfaction and rolled his back against the tree to reload. Like fat red wasps the Navajos' bullets zipped through the few dead leaves and limbs of the trees.

Zepko-eet-te and the boys drew in behind their trees. Zepko-eet-te heard White Wolf speaking from a great distance. "Get ready," the foggy voice said. Zepko-eet-te realized that he was part of the scene. He fitted an arrow into the curved horn bow. This was a battle, his battle.

As the morning light slipped down the walls and slowly filled the cañon, the Navajos moved out of the overhang and in among the boulders. White Wolf tried two more shots, but missed. The Navajos blistered the cottonwood grove in response.

"Where are our men?" asked one of the boys, ducking behind a splintered tree.

White Wolf glanced at the silent upper cañon, but said nothing.

They don't even shout encouragement to us, Zepko-eet-te said to himself. The men he had ridden out with were not what he had hoped for. With them we could make a good fight.

"We will make a good fight," White Wolf said, as if he had read Zepko-eet-te's mind.

Zepko-eet-te looked at their position. Only White Wolf had a gun. The boys had no weapons except knives. His own arrow quiver was nearly full but held less than two dozen arrows.

"Watch now!" White Wolf said. Zepko-eet-te looked at the camp. The Navajos were bringing up their horses. "They will circle us. You must keep the trees between you and the riders. Shoot when you can."

White Wolf was right. The Navajos rode boldly around the sheltering cottonwoods. The boys with no weapons simply crouched behind their trees and moved as the riders moved. A shot peeled bark near Zepko-eet-te's head. He crouched lower and followed the trotting circle. White Wolf pivoted around the rifle he held against the tree. He fired one shot, hitting the saddle tree of one of the riders. The Navajos rode back down the cañon.

"They are leaving," Bird-Seen-In-Winter shouted. "Hooray!"

White Wolf silently reloaded the heavy old rifle.

"They must reload, too," Zepko-eet-te said softly.

The boys became quiet.

Zepko-eet-te looked beyond his uncle at the silent, empty cañon where the other raiders hid. "Why do they not help us?"

White Wolf stood the rifle in position and sat waiting on his heels. He never looked toward the Kiowas hiding along the cañon walls. "We are not close with them. They came to take horses not to die."

"I thought all the People are brothers," Zepko-eet-te said.

White Wolf smiled softly. "All men are brothers, but all men are also men. And men often count the price of their own lives highly."

"Would you help them?" asked Zepko-eet-te.

"I like to fight," said White Wolf simply.

The Navajos returned, spinning their circle around the four trapped Kiowas. Zepko-eet-te raised up swiftly and placed an arrow deeply into one man's leg who lurched and kicked his horse forward down the cañon. The others followed.

The noon sun stood overhead before they came again. Zepko-eet-te spent several arrows that found no success. White Wolf fired once. There was a furious fusillade from the Navajos that penned the fighters tightly against the tree trunks. And then the enemy rode off again.

"Why didn't they come in?" asked Zepko-eet-te.

"They have time. When our ammunition is gone, they will not have to risk their lives," White Wolf answered.

Zepko-eet-te pulled two arrows from his quiver. One he held with his left hand against the bow. The other he fitted into the string.

The arrows were cruel works of a long and tedious art. Each dogwood shaft had been straightened and turned and dried and grooved and fitted meticulously with the man-killing points for his battles. Set horizontally into the shaft, the point would fly between a man's ribs. One corner was broken from each head — this modification Zepko-eet-te had learned from the seasoned warriors. It made the head sink deeply and twist. The Navajo he hit would have a bad time removing his Kiowa arrow.

The enemy came again. This time they spread their formation to stop the Kiowas from finding safety behind the trees. Again the gunfire came heavy. Zepko-eet-te lowered his head against the tree but raised his eyes to watch closely as the riders circled.

The crunch of leaves and limbs nearby caused Zepko-eet-te to turn. A wide-faced Navajo sat close in upon them, leveling his pistol at White Wolf. It exploded, throwing the Kiowa warrior back against the ground. White Wolf's own weapon discharged futilely into the air. The Navajo shouted and raised his gun high over his head. Zepko-eet-te loosed his arrow. It spun through the air into his enemy's chest. As the man gasped and wheeled away, he notched the second arrow into the string. The Navajo war party retreated.

Zepko-eet-te examined White Wolf's wound. The pistol ball had passed completely through his body. A clean hole showed where it entered and where it came out the other side. As he looked, the blood began to flow.

"They are back," White Wolf said. "Move."

White Wolf dragged himself behind a tree after the others. They all dodged bullets and tried to keep some cover between themselves and the attackers. Zepko-eet-te watched silently as his uncle staggered behind him. White Wolf kept his shield, but the heavy rifle slipped from his hands. The boys ducked frantically as the Navajos rode faster and closer. Shots kicked up around Zepko-eet-te's feet.

He alone was left to defend them. Yet his hands shook so furiously that he could not fit another arrow into the bow. He looked at the helpless boys. The triumphant faces of the Navajos rushed into his eyes and mind. He looked at White Wolf, dragging himself painfully between the trees and boulders. For a moment their eyes met.

White Wolf's once merry eyes looked deeply into Zepko-eet-te's doubt. "Do not give up. Try. Keep fighting back!" White Wolf slid down against the rock, unconscious.

Chapter Eleven

Zepko-eet-te felt the strength and power rise in him. He knew what to do. "Take my bow," he said to Finds-A-Coyote-Pup. "Bird-Seen-In-Winter, you help White Wolf lie down."

Zepko-eet-te had grabbed the rifle from where it had fallen and pulled the bloody powder horn from White Wolf's shoulder. Quickly he reloaded the weapon. His hands were steady. All time stopped. Zepko-eet-te moved as if there were no danger.

"When they come again, shoot at their horses. Horses are easier to hit than men."

Finds-A-Coyote-Pup raised the bow, prepared to do as Zepko-eet-te said. When the Navajos rode in again, both the boy and Zepko-eet-te fired at the horses. One went down hard, throwing the rider and rolling onto its side. Zepko-eet-te bent to reload quickly. The horse heaved out its life in a final lift of its side. The Navajos moved out of range.

"They will give us some room now," Zepko-eet-te said. "They cannot crowd us so close."

He sat, waiting, eyes fixed on the lower cañon. The Navajos sat out of range, talking. As he watched, he noticed the shadows had deepened. The cañon wall was again filling with darkness. The Navajos slowly turned and rode away down the cañon. Tomorrow, Zepko-eet-te

95

knew, they would return to finish the Kiowas — if they could.

Zepko-eet-te continued to watch where the Navajos had gathered. When he finally sat the old rifle on its butt, he was tired. But he was also disappointed. In the few minutes of his command he had discovered that he, like White Wolf, liked to fight. Without his noticing the long day had passed by — too quickly.

As soon as the last rider's hoof sounds disappeared from among the rocks, Zepko-eet-te went to White Wolf. "Boys, lift him to his feet. We must move now to another place." White Wolf struggled to assist the boys in helping him to his feet.

The four Kiowas began walking up the cañon, away from the Navajos, toward the hiding places of their own raiding party. Zepko-eet-te wondered if their men escaped unnoticed during the day's fighting. The men in the cottonwoods had heard nothing from them all day. Surely Catches Hold had led them away. Perhaps they had even hit the horse herd while the Navajos were busy with the four of them. Zepko-eet-te was young, but his mouth twisted in disgust at the other group's behavior. Such men! he thought.

White Wolf walked with great effort. Each step hurt him as the boys lifted and pulled him forward. A bright fresh flow of his blood issued from the wound. The trail it made would be easy to follow. Zepko-eet-te knew they must get to a safe place where the blood could be stanched and where a fight could be made.

Zepko-eet-te was now the leader of this helpless band; he thought only of their safety and of bringing them home. Horses and glory were gone from his mind, something for another day. A boy's dream of rich pleasure faded

Get Four Books Totally FREE* – A Value between $16 and $20

Tear here and mail your FREE* book card today!

in the strong light of a chief's trust.

A skitter of falling rocks from the cañon wall alerted Zepko-eet-te. He raised White Wolf's rifle and stepped between the boys and White Wolf and the noise.

"It is only I," called out Catches Hold. "We have been waiting for you."

Zepko-eet-te said nothing. He observed closely as the other members of Catches Hold's raiders rose up and stepped from the deep shadows of the boulders. In a little while the whole party reassembled around White Wolf and his three companions.

The boys helped White Wolf lie down within the protection of the boulders. He could no longer stand. The heavy sweat of weakness covered his hard, muscled body. Slowly the others sat down, too. Zepko-eet-te did not speak but waited for the toyapke to speak. Catches Hold sat silently. He still carried the pipe of his leadership. The men sat in complete silence for a very long time.

"Have the Navajos had enough, I want to know?" Old Crooked Man asked at last.

"No," said another Kiowa. "They will come back at first light."

Several of the other men agreed. But a few felt the danger from the Navajos was gone. "They lost two men and a horse and took away their surprise. That is enough for them," said one of the others.

"The raid is finished," said Old Crooked Man. "We cannot hope for horses now. It is best to go home quickly."

"The Navajos will think of that!" interjected Stands-Straight-Up. "They will catch us in the open as we try to return home."

Catches Hold did not speak at all. He seemed far removed from the discussion. Zepko-eet-te stared at the sand beyond his own knees. He leaned his head against White Wolf's rifle.

"What shall we do, Catches Hold?" someone asked.

Catches Hold looked at the group before him. "I have not thought on it yet. I have not decided."

"You are leader here," Old Crooked Man said. "It is your job to get us out of this situation."

"Yes," Summer Wanderer agreed. "The leader is responsible for his men."

There was silence as the men contemplated the desperate situation — Navajos ready to kill them, a leader who could not lead. Because Kiowa men went with a man they respected, they hesitated to confront him. They had, after all, chosen to follow Catches Hold. Before they would withdraw from a leader in a desperate place, they would think.

Zepko-eet-te did not speak. He listened, considered, waited. Quietly, distantly he observed. The rifle shaking in his grip caused him to look away from the deliberating men. The air was cold suddenly. Since he and the others had walked up the cañon, the temperature had fallen many degrees. When night finally filled the cañon, it would be very cold. He glanced at the tops of the cottonwoods. A strong breeze bent the trees before it. A norther!

Zepko-eet-te looked at the men around him. Not one had a blanket or a robe. They would freeze before morning — die without the help of the Navajos — unless they kept moving. They could keep alive only by walking.

The wounded man moaned softly as he moved his leg. White Wolf could not walk all night. He was a dead man even as they talked around him. Zepko-eet-te saw his uncle as a ghost among the living.

Zepko-eet-te stood up. His sudden movement startled the others as they sat deliberating. "There is a norther coming. I am going back to see if the Navajos left any robes or blankets. We are not safe from the Navajos here. Move up the cañon until you find a safe shelter. Do not leave White Wolf." He did not say because I will kill you if you do, but his soft words bore that threat. "Take him with you. I will find you again."

Zepko-eet-te turned and walked back down the cañon. When he came again to the camp site, he searched for blankets and food. The Navajos had left neither. Everything was gone. He sat down, listening to the cold wind pouring into the cañon, listening to his empty stomach. "I must find food and cover for White Wolf. I must find a way to carry him home alive to his sister, my mother."

Before the thought was complete, he remembered the horse killed in the afternoon's fight. He rose quickly and trotted to the cottonwood grove. He searched for the dead horse in the darkness until he stumbled over an outstretched foreleg. Kneeling near its belly, he raked together a handful of leaves and twigs. With flints and dried plant down from his fire bag he ignited a small fire and set about skinning and butchering the Navajo horse. He worked fast against the cold. He removed the hide and tossed chunks of meat into it. At last he gathered it together to form a sack and threw that onto his shoulder. He quenched the few embers of the fire and started back toward the others.

As *Zepko-eet-te* hurried up the cañon, the voice of the wind ran down the steep walls. It was a lonely voice full of discouragement — too much must be endured if the men were to get home again. The voice of fear penetrated the young man — give up, do not try to carry

99

so many weak men. You are not strong enough, young man.

Zepko-eet-te's own medicine voice remained silent as the boy listened to the other. Give me power to get White Wolf home, *he said to his Spirit.* I am tired. My heart is on the ground from these foolish men. Give me power, *Zepko-eet-te prayed.* Restore me. Show your care for me instead of being silent. You must speak louder than the other.

The cold voice of fear eased down the stone walls around Zepko-eet-te. "You grow weaker even as you walk," *it said.* "Your load is too heavy for so young a man. Feel the older men riding you down. You are far from your home."

Zepko-eet-te gripped the gathered horse hide tighter in his hands. But his arms ached. His feet seemed to move mere inches. He planted one hide-booted foot heavily and forced the other forward with his mind. The clothes that warmed him became lifeless weights as he bent forward into his climb. A numb foot slipped on the small glassy rocks. Still holding the meat sack tightly, he slid on his stomach and side back down the hill. The rocks scraped his hands and cut a gash in his cheek.

"Even a strong, young man grows weary. Even a young man's strength fails," *the wind said as the rocks pummeled his twisting body.*

Zepko-eet-te rode the slide down. Rocks struck the cold bony joints of his fingers with searing, grip-breaking pain. The makeshift sack opened, scattering the bloody meat. Zepko-eet-te watched as he and the meat slid apart. His body turned and twisted in the running rocks. He grabbed for a hold, but his frozen fingers could not catch. As he washed away in the rock avalanche, he saw his strength going up the cañon almost to the top, almost out of sight in the fresh moonlight.

No! *He searched with hands and feet and knees and thighs for a stopping grip. His left foot caught, and he grabbed at a bush beside him. It held. "I am Zepko-eet-te," he shouted in the face of the wind. "I am Zepko-eet-te . . . a warrior of the People. My father is Big Bow, a brave man. My grandfather was Big Bow, a brave man. I am their son. My blood is strong. I will not quit here. I will not quit."*

"Where is your medicine?" the wind whistled in his face.

Before Zepko-eet-te could answer, he heard a whinny. He raised himself on his bruised forearms and turned onto his side to look about. Above him he saw the moon's cool circle beyond the cañon wall. Her clear soothing rays fell into the cañon cathedral. Below him the light ran down the path and illuminated a side cañon he had walked past in the darkness with his burden, and in the depth of the cañon alcove he saw a white-striped face with ears upright and forward — a horse.

The filly stood still, feet together, chest against a single corral pole, as the stones around her dropped across the opening. She raised her head a few inches and lowered it again as if she could not believe her eyes. The warrior blinked and sat up. As he rose, the horse put her head forward, eager for this companion on the lonely, moon-touched mountain. Raising his shirt and unwrapping the lariat wound about his waist, Zepko-eet-te walked toward her. He made a halter and pulled away the corral pole. The horse stepped forward. He stroked her strong jaw and warmed his face briefly against her neck.

Zepko-eet-te, something said within him. This is your

medicine . . . to step out without trinkets or images men carry about. Be strong in yourself. I have made you complete. Your courage will draw my power.

In the moonlight Zepko-eet-te found scattered pieces of horse meat and the fresh hide. He again gathered the meat in the hide, cut a tying strip, and bound the sack securely together. Mounting the horse, he let her pick the trail up the cañon.

Zepko-eet-te came again to the place where he had left the others and rode on, listening for their sounds, looking for the little fire they would build. There was only silence and moonlit darkness and the sound of the mare's small hoofs.

Zepko-eet-te called out to the shadows. "Where are you?"

No answer came.

Again Zepko-eet-te called. "Men of the People, where are you?" He sat still, listening, watching the horse move her ears to listen with him.

"Here," a feeble voice said from the darkness. "Here."

Zepko-eet-te slipped from the horse to find White Wolf. His anger rose as he searched for his uncle. When the other men saw that the rider was Zepko-eet-te, they came out of hiding. The boy found his uncle in the deep shadows beside the trail as the men gathered around him.

"They left you," he said bitterly.

White Wolf gripped his arm weakly. He spoke so feebly that Zepko-eet-te had to lean very close to hear. "But one man also found me," he said.

"Did you find food and blankets?" the men asked. Their voices seemed loud and false in the stillness.

Zepko-eet-te forced down his anger at their self-seeking interest. A leader must know this quality of men, too.

"There were no blankets," he said as he moved White Wolf back against the boulders.

The shivering men stood around, waiting as Zepko-eet-te built a small fire. He brought the skin bag from his horse and started to hang strips of raw meat near the fire. "You may eat this meat, and we have water."

As the meat cooked, the men sat silently about the fire and waited. Zepko-eet-te watched their faces, and his anger cooled. Men were but feeble creatures, all voice and little strength, he thought. No food or shelter, no one to lead them, and they became small and puny.

He took the water paunch the boys placed near him and wet a piece of cloth. In the light of the fire he washed White Wolf's wounds. He heated tallow from the ball he carried in his medicine bag and poured it into the wound. The simple ministrations soothed White Wolf, and he ate a little of the tough roast meat and drank a cupful of water.

As White Wolf ate and rested, Zepko-eet-te dug a long narrow hole in the sand. More and more it resembled a shallow grave. The men watched intently. Surely the young man would not dig his uncle's grave in front of him. Zepko-eet-te spoke to no one. He gathered dry grass and lined the hole. When he had finished, he carried White Wolf to the hole and laid him gently onto the sweet smelling grass. He covered him with more grass, and then lay down beside him. He pulled the horse hide over them both. The boys quickly dug a pit and filled it with grass and lay down together beneath a scant layer of grass and leaves.

The wind grew. The fire slowly burned itself down to ember and ash. "We need more wood," said Stands-Straight-Up.

"No, the Navajos will see the fire," said Summer Wanderer.

Gradually the men crowded near the bed where White Wolf and Zepko-eet-te lay. One tried to lift the hide corner and slip beneath. Zepko-eet-te sat up. "I am tired of this. You are men of the People, not children. Remember yourselves. You must walk to keep warm, or you must dig holes and gather what cover you can. These children shame you. They have made a place for themselves. Do the same. Morning will come."

A light blanket of snow had now covered the stiff horse hide that protected Zepko-eet-te and White Wolf. The dry flakes spilled away as the young man lifted the skin and sat up. He pulled back the hide gently to reveal White Wolf's colorless face. White Wolf opened his eyes and looked wearily at Zepko-eet-te. Zepko-eet-te smiled. His uncle lived. The boy had brought this man to another day.

Zepko-eet-te looked at the men around him, huddled together, sleepless, miserable. He noted the snow-heavy sky, and he knew, just as he knew his own name, that the Navajos would not come again. The enemy was gone.

"Boy," he said to Bird-Seen-In-Winter. "Build a fire and cook the meat."

Zepko-eet-te left his bed and pulled the cover back over White Wolf. He stretched the bruised stiffness of his own body. The two boys worked, gathering wood. The men sat still and lifeless.

"You, men of the People," Zepko-eet-te spoke quietly. "I am going home. If you follow me, I will lead you safely home. If anyone has an objection, now is the best time to make it."

The men remained silent. Not even Catches Hold spoke out against Zepko-eet-te. As the fire caught, they moved closer. Zepko-eet-te studied them for any hidden dissent.

"Good," said the young leader. "Here is my plan. The Navajos will not come here. They will stay warm and comfortable today. But, when the weather is to their liking, they will seek to catch us in the open on our return journey. They will think of the rising river. They will expect us to go upstream to find a ford. We will go downstream and cross far below our raiding camp. It will be a long, hard journey to the river and across. But we will cross."

"What if you mis-think the Navajos? We will walk a long way and take many chances for nothing," Old Crooked Man said as he chewed a strip of the nearly raw horse meat. Two of Catches Hold's followers nodded agreement.

"It is a dangerous plan," Summer Wanderer added.

"It is a plan," Stands-Straight-Up said. The men became silent. "It is a plan."

Zepko-eet-te won. Power came to him. He would carry the burden. He had the boys fasten the horse hide to poles for a litter. As they worked, he fed and tended White Wolf. Together he and the boys laid the wounded man on the sling. They began the journey home.

The party of Kiowas traveled silently along the side of a ridge that ran in a southeasterly direction back toward the Pecos. They never revealed themselves against the sky but stayed high on the side of the ridge so they could see any enemy from a great distance. They switched bearers on White Wolf's litter many times during the long day. They rested little and ate nothing. Moving as fast as they could, they remained merely men on foot. Riders could easily overtake them.

Zepko-eet-te scouted ahead of the main party on the horse he had found. Before nightfall he located a safe camp site and built a fire for the others. He sat, cooking the remaining horse meat, when the men came in. Each came quickly to the fire for the world had grown cold again in the twilight. As they sat down beside Zepko-eet-te, they saw there was little meat. Their stomachs rumbled as they silently counted the meat and the men. Zepko-eet-te sliced the largest portion for White Wolf and fed him quietly as the others ate what was left.

"Kill the horse," said Catches Hold. "Her meat will satisfy our twisting bellies and give us strength to travel on. Without food we will become too weak to walk."

Zepko-eet-te looked at Catches Hold, at the hungry men around him. "No," he said quietly. "Come close and listen to me. I know that you are hungry. I am hungry, too. But we are only a little hungry. We have been hungry before. This horse is not food."

Catches Hold threw down his quiver and sat abruptly. "You are the leader."

"The leader," said Stands-Straight-Up.

"Umph," said Old Crooked Man, and spat at the fire. But no man stood against Zepko-eet-te for the horse.

Without food and with little warmth the night was long. The moaning of Summer Wanderer made the night longer.

"Why are you groaning?" asked Zepko-eet-te.

"I am shot in the head. The Navajos' last attack. I was hit in the forehead. Look at the blood," said Summer Wanderer.

"White Wolf is shot all the way through his body, and he does not make the noise you make," Zepko-eet-te said.

Summer Wanderer fell silent. Zepko-eet-te lay back. Soon the moans began again.

106

"I do not understand this," Zepko-eet-te said to White Wolf. "This man was not in the fight but stayed far up the cañon. The Navajos shot at us in the cottonwoods. They would have to be strange shots to hit Summer Wanderer way up the cañon behind a boulder. Tomorrow we will find the truth . . . if the Navajos don't kill us first."

Chapter Twelve

Zepko-eet-te had waked before dawn. He cleaned and dressed White Wolf's wound. He woke the boys. "I'm going on ahead. I may be able to kill something to eat before our stomachs grow to our spines. Follow my tracks. Do not let the men leave this wounded one." He rode away on the little filly.

The raiders walked only two hours when they heard a rifle shot. "He has killed something to eat," said Catches Hold. "This way." He ran toward the sound of the report. The other men forgot their tiredness and began to run after him. The men spread out as they ran. The swifter ones took the lead.

Only the boys and three men remained around White Wolf. "Take my place," said Stands-Straight-Up. "I have walked a long way with the litter." And he went away, too.

Zepko-eet-te had killed two does with arrows he had collected from among the men in the raiding party. He had fired the rifle as a signal for the others. This encouragement would keep them walking, walking faster. He skinned the carcasses and was roasting the meat on the fire when he saw the first runners coming toward his sheltered camp. He rose quickly to his feet.

"Catches Hold, where is White Wolf?" he asked.

"Oh, they are carrying him along. We have carried him

by turns. It is slow to carry a man. Two deer." Catches Hold fixed his attention on the meal. "Small, but two is good." His eyes were on the meat, and he did not see the concern in the young chief's eyes.

Zepko-eet-te stood waiting for the others. One by one they came in and dropped near the fire. Four figures carrying the litter finally appeared a long way in the distance. Catches Hold stepped up beside Zepko-eet-te. "Could we begin eating now?" he asked.

"The food is to eat," said Zepko-eet-te, as he walked out to meet his uncle. He caught one of the boy's shoulders as he passed. "You are men already. Uncle, there is food and rest ahead."

When White Wolf had eaten, Zepko-eet-te sat with his own food. "My head is so painful," Summer Wanderer complained. As he ate, Zepko-eet-te studied the man closely. He had been among the first to reach the breakfast camp in spite of his wound that had bothered the whole party throughout the night. Summer Wanderer continued his complaint. "The wound is so tender. Just touching it, even the air touching it, brings pain."

Zepko-eet-te looked at the dark swollen bruise near Wanderer's hairline. Blood from the wound had dried on his forehead and had fallen away piecemeal. Zepko-eet-te noted scratches near the bruise. He thought he saw something protruding from the wounded flesh. "Summer Wanderer, my grandfather and father taught me much about wounds. It may be I can help you," Zepko-eet-te said as he ate.

"You seem to know everything," said Summer Wanderer. "No man can know everything. Not even you, Zepko-eet-te. I do not want your doctoring. I will bear my pain alone."

Zepko-eet-te glanced at the litter bearers who were alert to the conversation. Looking directly at them, not at Summer Wanderer, he said: "But you do not suffer alone. We were all kept awake by your pain. I'm sure there are many here who will help me with your healing." With the last words Zepko-eet-te reached across the fire toward Summer Wanderer who withdrew speedily into the grips of the four young men and boys.

"You will kill me!" Summer Wanderer cried. "Just to keep me quiet, you will kill me. I have had many troubles, but I am still a Kiowa like you. It is wrong to kill me because I am inconvenient for you."

Zepko-eet-te and the others began to laugh. "Kill you, Summer Wanderer, for whimpering like a puppy? I will help you," Zepko-eet-te said.

As his hand moved toward the wound, Wanderer turned his head away. Zepko-eet-te grasped his jaws firmly and turned the wound toward him. "Hold him." One of the young men caught Summer Wanderer's head firmly by the ears. Zepko-eet-te reached into his sewing pouch and brought out his awl. Wanderer followed his movements with frantic eyes. But before he could protest again, Zepko-eet-te split open the wound and dug out a sliver of wood. He held it where Wanderer could see. "Here is your bullet!" Zepko-eet-te stood up. "You ran into a limb when you ran away. A bullet would have been in your other end!"

The Kiowas began to laugh. Even Summer Wanderer laughed shyly. "That is true, Zepko-eet-te. I don't think I will save this bullet for my wife." He tossed the wood fragment into the fire.

Full bellies and laughter helped the men regain their hearts. Zepko-eet-te's way was easy in his teasing. "Shall

110

we make another litter, Summer Wanderer, or can you make it from here?" Zepko-eet-te laughed. The laughter came to all again.

"I will only lean a little on White Wolf," Summer Wanderer said, laughing too.

"Good, I count on you Summer Wanderer," Zepko-eet-te said. "We must move on now. I will see you in the evening."

Zepko-eet-te left to ride before the others. In an hour the others followed his trail across the winter land toward the river. He killed more deer and left the carcasses for them to skin and butcher. Before nightfall each pair of men had a hide to share.

Zepko-eet-te rode far ahead of the others, looking at the land, searching for any Navajo who might try to cut off their escape. As he rode into a small meadow, he jerked the horse up tight and sat looking at a herd of horses — all hobbled. The raiders, mounted double, could ride home. Zepko-eet-te sat astonished until he remembered. "Be strong in yourself. Your courage will draw my power."

Leaning down and cutting the leather or rope hobbles, he rode quietly among the animals. He silently edged them back over his trail away from the owners who must lie somewhere ahead.

As the distance from the owners increased, so did Zepko-eet-te's joy. When he felt safe, Zepko-eet-te shouted loudly. Throwing his head back and his arms toward the sky, he rode around the herd. He was his father's son. He drove the gather before him with his coat. They galloped toward the walking Kiowas.

When the men saw the horse herd coming toward them with Zepko-eet-te waving his coat, they too shouted. They

111

quickly unwrapped their lariats and caught the ponies.

"Zepko-eet-te, your medicine is very strong," said Summer Wanderer. "I will be happier riding any horse than walking."

The men helped White Wolf from his litter and lifted him onto a horse. Bird-Seen-In-Winter sat behind him.

"Hold him fast," Zepko-eet-te said. "He is a great man of the People. Go on now. You, Elk's Blood and Reflects-Like-A-Mirror, ride our back trail. Hobbled horses belong to someone. We will be followed."

So the raiding party rode with their backs to the sun toward the Pecos and safety. In the night camp they cooked more of the deer meat and settled in pairs beneath the raw skins.

Zepko-eet-te sat long after dressing White Wolf's wound, long after the others slept. There was much to think about in order to save the other men.

Zepko-eet-te's scouts came in quietly as he sat before the fire.

"The Navajos are scouting for white soldiers and some ranchers," Reflects-Like-A-Mirror said.

"They cannot follow us at night," Zepko-eet-te said. "Eat what is cooked." The scouts took meat from the spit and sat down to eat. Zepko-eet-te waited. "How far behind are these men?"

Elk's Blood looked up from his eating. "We have maybe half a day on them."

Zepko-eet-te thought of the small amount of time and the distance of the river. "Good. We must get off very early, then. You two remain in the rear again." He thought a moment. "Keep me in sight. When first you see the enemy, signal and come quickly. We must cross the river before we can turn for home."

112

Two enemies were now at their backs, the Navajos and the soldiers, the white men whose horses he had taken. The Pecos was half a day ahead. Zepko-eet-te must decide before morning whether to split the party, putting each man on his own, or to keep them moving together. White Wolf would slow them down. There would be no time to waste concealing their tracks. Tomorrow would be a race for the river.

Chapter Thirteen

The main Kiowa party sighted the river at mid-morning. Zepko-eet-te sat on a rise, looking at the river. "Go on," he said to the others. "I will watch here." He waited for them to pass down toward the distant river and then turned his horse back to watch for the men left behind.

Before long Zepko-eet-te saw the tiny dots that were his two scouts. They rode a wide circle against the side of a roll in the land. Zepko-eet-te knew immediately that the enemy was in sight and searching for the raiders' trail. He spun the filly and laid the whip to her side. She shot forward after the others. Zepko-eet-te yelled as he rode. The men ahead began to run toward the river.

The fleet pony brought him quickly into the galloping party of double-mounted men. White Wolf's face was gray, full of pain and weariness. But he rode as hard as the rest. Zepko-eet-te stayed just behind him. The river grew larger as the men rode, but, until the heaving horses stopped on the banks, Zepko-eet-te could not judge its danger.

The filly's sides moved hard beneath his legs as Zepko-eet-te surveyed the turbulent water. The river ran out seventy-five, perhaps eighty, yards. There was no time to seek a ford. A ford would not matter with the flood swollen by melted snow and rain anyway. Debris, bobbing, disappearing, and reappearing further down the river, *floated on the swirling surface. A cold wind blew hard against Zepko-eet-te as he made his plan.*

"Bird-Seen-In-Winter, build a float." The men looked at Zepko-eet-te as he spoke. "Put White Wolf on it and put it into the water. Hold it fast. I'll be back in a little while and take him across. The rest of you, get your horses into the water and go over the river now."

Zepko-eet-te went back over the lip of the river bank to check on the enemy. He dropped from the pony into the mesquite. Reflects-Like-A-Mirror and Elk's Blood crossed the remaining ground to the river and skidded in beside Zepko-eet-te. Standing, without greeting, he slapped the near horse's rump and sent the scouts on to the river. "Go on, get across," he shouted.

As the last two men rode into the river bottom, the boat builders worked at gathering the brush caught and growing on the collapsing bank. They drew it into a tight pile beneath a deer skin and bound it securely with a leather lariat. White Wolf crawled onto the float. The boys pushed it into the edge of the current. Still the remaining raiders sat, looking at the wide treachery before them.

The sound of Zepko-eet-te's rifle caused them to look around. The young chief fired at the approaching riders and ran, reloading, to another shooting position. Twice more he fired and ran, trying to make the advancing enemy deploy.

"Take cover," he said to them, panting. "There are many guns up here. Many guns shooting. See the smoke." He ran, fired, and looked at the enemy who pulled up at last and sought cover. "So," said Zepko-eet-te, "maybe that will hold you for a while."

The young warrior flung himself onto the pony and dashed back to the river. Those of his men who had not crossed still sat on the near bank. "Get into the water," he shouted above the river's roar. He signaled to them. "Go."

Their timidity angered Zepko-eet-te, but his mind turned quickly to White Wolf. Zepko-eet-te jumped to the ground near White Wolf's raft. He pushed the boys toward his horse and the river. "Go," he said to them. Zepko-eet-te stripped off his coat and laid it with the rifle and his necessities beside White Wolf. He flung his arm in a harsh signal to the others. "Move out," he shouted.

Zepko-eet-te did not wait. He caught the line to the raft and stepped into the icy water. The water swirled against him, staggered him, sucked away his breath. He had no more words. The struggle to stay on his feet consumed all his efforts. Towing the raft, he waded into the deepening current past his knees, past his thighs. He walked on, fighting the current, staying on his feet, until he could no longer touch the sandy bottom. The current took him. He began to swim, using the current, driving his strong arms into the freezing water, kicking from the buttocks with all his young strength. He breathed hard, concentrating on stroking the water.

Zepko-eet-te lost sight of the distant shore, but still he stroked and kicked, stroked and kicked, until his chest and chin cut into the sandy bank. His hand shot out, grabbing for a hold, losing it, grabbing again. He struggled to his feet and pulled the raft with him. As the raw wind drove over the empty land against his clothing, his teeth chattered. He dragged the raft out of the water and pulled White Wolf onto the dry ground. Together they struggled on across the muddy flat toward cover.

At last Zepko-eet-te lay White Wolf upon the land and fell to his knees among the flotsam. He placed his coat

116

over White Wolf. With shaking fingers Zepko-eet-te chopped a spark from his flints into a tinder fire. He gathered more small limbs and looked up as the filly leaped out of the river, followed by the shivering boys.

Zepko-eet-te looked for the others. The men still sat on the far bank. "Drive your horses into the river," he shouted, unheard above the current. "Swim the horses. Hold their tails." Still they sat, and then, suddenly, the horses leaped forward into the raging water.

Zepko-eet-te watched silently by the fire. White Wolf raised himself on one elbow to see the desperate men fighting their way across. The great strength of the horses was small against the river. But the men could only hold on and let the animals struggle. One by one the horses crossed and plunged up the bank. The exhausted men fell, gasping, onto the land, then came shivering, half dead, to the fire.

Zepko-eet-te let them warm themselves as he watched the far bank. He saw movement on that side, and kicked the fire apart. The Kiowa men screamed at him. "Move out," he shouted.

"We are freezing," Summer Wanderer growled.

Zepko-eet-te shoved one of the men. "Help White Wolf!"

Zepko-eet-te pulled Summer Wanderer to his feet and pushed him forward. "Go on. We are too easily good targets here. Go on." The young chief picked up a mesquite limb and raised it. "Must I force you to save your life?"

From the other side of the river several shots skipped over the whirling surface of the water. The raiders dragged themselves sullenly off the shore toward the mesquite thicket. Zepko-eet-te stayed, waited for the pursuers to cross. The enemy men, white and red, ranged up and down the far shore, looking at the icy water, shouting at each other. Then they stopped, dismounted, and began firing toward the far side. Zepko-eet-te smiled and trotted into the mesquite after the others.

"Let's get going," he said, as he joined the others. "It is not safe to stop. Finds-A-Coyote-Pup and Bird-Seen-In-Winter, ride north to the base camp and tell the baggage boys to bring the horses and supplies to Muchaque." The boys caught a horse and struggled, shivering, aboard. "Let's go."

"We are wet. We are freezing. We must have a fire, Zepko-eet-te," Summer Wanderer pleaded.

"Walking and running will make you dry and warm. Lead the horses," Zepko-eet-te said, as he helped White Wolf onto the filly and wrapped a deer skin over his shoulders. "You must ride." He put on his own coat. "I will lead."

Summer Wanderer threw his shield at Zepko-eet-te. "I will not go one step more. I want a fire." Three other men joined him in the confrontation. Zepko-eet-te stood still. Only Elk's Blood and Reflects-Like-A-Mirror stepped up beside him.

Zepko-eet-te heard a voice above him say: "You men listen to me." White Wolf spoke weakly but clearly. "You have whined enough. This man is not your enemy. He wants to save your lives. Stop complaining and quarreling. He will bring you home. Act worthy of yourselves."

The men looked at White Wolf, gaunt and pale, steadying himself over the horse's wet, shining withers. Catches Hold dropped his gaze. One by one the others realized their shame.

Catches Hold stepped forward, picked up Summer Wanderer's shield, and handed it back to him. "You are right, White Wolf. The boy has succeeded where I have failed.

I have not cared for my men. I have worked against them when I resisted this man. Zepko-eet-te, I will follow you home. You are now toyapke, leader."

He handed the pipe to the young chief. Leading his horse, Catches Hold walked briskly toward home. The others trotted after. As Zepko-eet-te watched them, his uncle leaned forward and grasped his shoulder. "Toyapke, take us home."

Chapter Fourteen

Daha-hen's children were asleep long before he finished his story. Across the fire the young men were very quiet. All their lives they had heard that Daha-hen had become a chief before his eighteenth summer and had gone on to become a great warrior. Now he himself had shared his story. In the telling he had set their futures before them, as Kiowa men had done for the young men of many generations. Each heart beat with the glory of the People. Each thought of his own place among them.

Thomas stood up as Daha-hen left the arbor. He followed him out into the night. Daha-hen stroked the neck of his horse, ran his hand down the back, and along each leg before lifting a hoof. He said: "In the free time it was a great honor to take a horse tied to the owner's leg or lodge. Once, when I was a young man, I went into a Ute camp and took three horses. People do not think so much of horses now. Good night, Thomassey. Throw your blanket wherever you like under the arbor."

Thomas Young Man watched Daha-hen go into the arbor, strip off his white man's clothes, and lie down. He walked to his little pony. It grazed the long grass beside Daha-hen's horse. It was a good pony, the boy thought, a good pony. Not much to look at, no black ears, thin, but its heart was good. It had come all the way from Anadarko without any trouble. It would go farther. He pulled the horse's head to him and looked into the big eyes.

"You are my horse," he said. "You are a fine horse. Your heart is good." Thomas stroked the muzzle, then let the little animal return to its busy grazing. He ran his hand over it as he had seen Daha-hen do.

Thomas looked into the sky . The moon was growing full. There, above him, were the seven Kiowa sisters and their brother, the Bear. "Everything has a place," he whispered to himself. "Everything has a place, but Thomas Young Man." He stood silently, looking at the sky. "But a man can make a place for himself if his heart is very brave."

At last, taking his blanket from his saddle beside the arbor, he went inside and lay down. The other boys took no notice of him.

When Elk, Broken Stick, and Gnat Catcher went down to the creek in the morning, Thomas Young Man stood with the little horse in the water. He wrung a cloth and let water trickle over the pony's back, then wiped it dry with the edge of a stick.

"Go and get my bow," said Elk. "That looks like a buffalo calf to me. I will kill it, and we will eat it together."

"That is too much trouble," said Loud Talker's son. "Just drive him out of the water so that our horses can drink."

Elk shied a stone at Thomas's horse. "Get that mutt out of the water, *dapom.* We want to water our horses."

Thomas rested an arm on the horse's back. "The creek is long, Elk. Do you want upstream or downstream?"

"I want you and your cahoose out," said Elk. He threw another stone, hitting the little horse on the rump, caus-

121

ing it to kick. He laughed. The other boys picked up stones and chunked them at Thomas and his horse. Thomas ducked down behind the pony.

"Ha," said Elk, "that is something the stupid creature is good for."

Thomas put his head in his hands. A rock hit the pony. It squealed. *This is enough*, thought Thomas Young Man. *I will not stand for this.* He reached into his pocket.

Elk bent to pick up another rock. As he straightened, a rock cut across his cheekbone, knocking him backwards onto his behind. "Heh-up. What's going on?"

A missile struck Gnat Catcher in the chest. "What's he trying to do?" he said, backing away.

The hurled stones sung by the boys' ears, and they began to give ground. Thomas jumped onto the back of his pony and spun him out of the water and up the hill toward them. In his raised arm he swung a leather thong with a heavy rock set in the pocket. Elk and the others quickly took to their horses.

"What's the matter with you?" shouted Elk as Thomas rode closer. "What's the matter with him?" he asked his companions. "At the agency he is a whipped dog."

"I am not at the agency now," Thomas said, drawing up and taking the slingshot into his lap. "This is open country . . . Kiowa country. I have as much right here as anyone. Try me again, Elk, and I will shoot your eye out."

"You are too angry," the older boy said.

Thomas sat a moment, cooling his thoughts and words. "You have heard my words, Elk," he said, and trotted the little pony back toward the camp. He stopped beside Daha-hen who had been sitting on his horse, watching the boy fighting.

122

"The Methodists?" Daha-hen asked

Thomas ducked his head and smiled. "Little David and Goliath," he said. "First Samuel Seventeen."

"Little David of the two hundred foreskins?" Daha-hen asked. Thomas nodded. "Hmm. I hope you will not take this thing too far, Thomassey."

"Daha-hen," Thomas said, drawing himself up, "I would like to go after the horse thieves with you."

"I accept you, Thomas Young Man," the *toyapke* said.

Chapter Fifteen

Five riders left Daha-hen's camp and rode north and west along the trail of the Gambler and the white horse thieves. Daha-hen rode, without looking at the trail, to the river crossing where two days before he had stopped. This time he plunged his pony into the water and rode freely out the other side. Elk and the other boys whooped when they broke the boundary. This was Kiowa country again.

Daha-hen set the pace after crossing the north fork of the Red River above Elk Creek. The Gambler's trail was easy to follow — a wide trail of many horses and men. The boys rode silently in a line behind the warrior.

The rough, hilly country gradually gave way to high, elevated plains. As Thomas looked back, he could see a great vista, stretching away for many miles, revealing in the far distance the rising peaks of the Wichita Mountains. The People were there, going about their day, not knowing, not caring that some Kiowas were again on the plains in pursuit of their enemies.

Travel on the plains is ever-changing, yet never changes. Depressions, ravines, cañons, each varied from the last yet very like the last, rise constantly before the traveler. Looking over the plains, the topographical features are not visible, and then with sudden abruptness the rider comes upon them.

A constant optical illusion from the atmosphere and deflected perspective of the plains makes judging distance impossible. What seems near turns out to be far away — a day's ride perhaps. And when the mind realizes the eye's error and begins to see the distance is great, the rider is right upon what he thought was miles away.

"I think he knows where they are going already," whispered Broken Stick. "I am sure it is not far."

Elk said: "It may well be he knows. My uncle knows this country very well and also the ways of men. Now be quiet."

"I hope it is not far," Broken Stick groused.

"Quiet," said Elk. "It is as far as it is. That is all. It is as far as it is."

"We've already ridden many miles, many hours," complained Broken Stick. "It cannot be far."

Thomas's stomach began to gnaw long before noon, but he rode without saying anything. Thomas had been hungry before — many times. Sometimes he had fought the dogs for thrown-out bones. Sometimes a woman left him something outside the teepee. Many times he curled himself in the corner of a building and fell asleep, dreaming of the food he would someday have in abundance. That was when he was a very little boy, when his mother had forgotten him for the soldiers and the whiskey. She never ate.

But the Methodists always had food, good food. Even among themselves they were famous for food. Thomas thought of the big breakfasts of eggs and pancakes, covered with syrup, and meat and coffee and milk. He never was hungry with the Methodists. The cook was always putting more food on his plate, and he was always eating it, eating it, filling his emptiness. He smiled.

125

"When are we going to stop to eat?" asked Gnat Catcher.

"Quiet," said Elk who rode nearest Daha-hen.

"Eat the dried meat in your bags," said Daha-hen. "We will not stop to eat."

The boys dug in the small bags that Many Tongues had given them when they left. Daha-hen did not eat, Thomas saw, and put away the jerked meat he was about to put in his mouth.

Throughout the long afternoon the warrior led them, trotting and walking, along the thieves' trail. At last Daha-hen pulled up, causing the boys to bump into each other. He sat on his pony at the top of a rise. The others looked where he looked and saw nothing but more broken country.

"We are leaving the trail for a while," said Daha-hen. "We will find it again on the other side of the small-oak country."

He kicked the pony off the rise and rode into the massive forest of miniature oaks barely more than a foot or two high, yet some still laden with last season's acorns. The boys followed, allowing the horses to thread their ways among the oaks.

Coming out of the passage at last, the Kiowas rode, looking at the ground until Daha-hen again found the fugitives' trail. It seemed to the young men that Daha-hen had no trouble finding the trail and anticipating the path of the thieves. Twice more during the afternoon they left the wide trail, cut across country, and found it again at streams or narrow defiles through the rocks.

At the streams Daha-hen let the horses and boys drink and rest briefly. He never spoke, took small notice of them. If he thought them fit or unfit, he never said.

When he judged the rest sufficient, he remounted and rode away. The boys struggled atop their ponies and followed.

"Can't he talk?" asked Broken Stick.

"Shut up," answered Elk.

"He makes me very nervous. I just relax, and he rides off without a word," Broken Stick continued. "I keep thinking he'll get tired, but he keeps going. I'm about to fall off my horse, I'm so tired."

The constant wind of the plains cooled them, but the heat hung over them as they rode into the long afternoon. They left the broken country and came up onto the sandy hills cut on top with deep gullies where the ceaseless wind ever moved the sand.

"*Hoodlety! Hoodlety!* Hurry! Hurry!" shouted Daha-hen, pointing at something behind them.

The boys twisted and looked back at what he saw behind them. The head wind had shifted, picked up the sand, and hurled it into the sky to chase them, sting them. A faint cloud ran from the horizon toward them.

Daha-hen put his horse into a slow lope, and the others followed. But the wind and sand were faster than men and horses. Sand and small pebbles soon stung their ears and the sides of their faces, stuck to the exposed parts of their sweating bodies. The horses fought and pitched under the constant noise and pelting and the hard hands of their riders.

With the wind and sand at their backs the five riders held their course, but they groped slowly now through the dust-filled air, unable to see objects within a few feet of them. Their noses and eyes and ears and mouths filled with dust.

Daha-hen led them into a gully. Pulling their blankets

over their heads and their horses' heads, they waited for the sand storm to pass at last over them. A man must sometimes step aside to let nature pass.

Broken Stick and Gnat Catcher spit the sand from their mouths and wiped their faces, glaring at Elk. Thomas felt the grit in his back teeth. He rubbed his eyes. His little horse had thick sand in its long lashes. He gently brushed it away and wiped the great, tearing eyes. Before he was back on his horse, Daha-hen had ridden out of the gully and was again in pursuit of the thieves.

This time Thomas rode forward, leaving Elk, Gnat Catcher, and Broken Stick grumbling as they remounted their ponies. They did not notice.

"When will we stop again?" asked Gnat Catcher. "I am still tired. I need to get the sand out of my clothes."

"Shut up," said Elk. "You are not a child. You chose to come along."

"I did not know it would take so long," said Broken Stick.

"They are two days ahead of us," reasoned Elk. "Now come on. You have put us behind that *dapom*."

Broken Stick threw himself into the saddle. "Two days. Two whole days." He bumped Gnat Catcher aside as he rode up behind Elk.

"I'm not sure I want to put my horse through much more of this," Broken Stick grumbled. "He is a valuable horse. I do not want to waste him in a hopeless pursuit through rough country."

"Shut up," said Elk.

128

Chapter Sixteen

As the afternoon progressed, a sense grew in the boys that the pursuit was not hopeless. They had a growing sense that the warrior who rode before them would inevitably find his enemies. Daha-hen was as constant and steady as the ceaseless wind. He would not quit.

"We will ride all night," Daha-hen said, drawing up, a silhouette against the glow of the setting sun. "You can eat now and drink. Tonight, tie yourselves to your horses and sleep, if you must. Do not fall behind in the darkness." He turned and rode on. Thomas followed.

"Doesn't that old man ever quit?" asked Gnat Catcher. "The sand in my clothes has worn sores on me. I must get it out of my clothes right now." He stopped his pony and jumped to the ground.

"Do not fall behind." Elk circled about him fearfully. "He will not come back for you."

"I don't care," said Gnat Catcher. "Do you hear, I do not care! I'm tired. I am covered with sand and sores. I have ridden a very long way with a crazy man."

"Quiet," said Elk. "He will hear you."

"I do not care," said Gnat Catcher.

"As long as you are stopping, so will I." Broken Stick dropped from his horse and began to strip off his clothes. "You have a good idea, Gnat Catcher."

Elk said nothing but joined his friends in shaking the

129

sand from his clothes. When the three had redressed, he called out: "Let's go. We can catch up quickly." He rode away as the other two slowly remounted and followed.

The sunset lingered a long time, fading from oranges and blues into purples and, finally, blackness. Daha-hen let his horse walk until the moon rose and covered the land with its pale light. Then he began to trot again.

"How can anyone sleep on a trotting horse?" asked Elk.

"Your uncle does not sleep," answered Thomas softly.

"Neither does anyone else," said Elk.

"How! How! Yes! Yes!" agreed Gnat Catcher and Broken Stick.

The boys rode on in the moonlight behind Daha-hen. When the horses walked, they fell forward on their necks and rested. Sometimes they fell asleep only to be awakened again as their ponies took up the trot again behind the indefatigable Daha-hen.

Thomas slumped over the pony's neck, dozing in the cool night. *Don't feed that dapom again,"* the man said in his dream. *The woman looked down and went back into the teepee. The man threw a stick at the small fleeing boy, hitting him solidly in the back. "Get out of here. Don't come back. You don't live here any more. That one will never amount to anything,"* he said to the woman.

Thomas sat up. He felt tears on his cheeks and brushed them quickly away. He shook himself hard, trying to get rid of the dream and his remaining sleepiness. Finally he rode up beside Daha-hen.

"Is it wrong to talk now?" the boy asked.

"Yes," said Daha-hen.

"It will keep us awake," the boy said.

130

"I am already awake." Daha-hen stretched in the saddle. He looked closely at the son of Young Man and Yellow Walking Woman. "Many men sleep in the saddle. It is acceptable on a long trail."

"I do not want to sleep," confessed Thomas. "I want to measure up. I am afraid that I will fall away and be left behind."

"Your horse will keep up like the others," Daha-hen stated. "Do not worry about that."

"No," the boy said. "I do not want to miss anything."

"Now there is nothing to miss," the man said. "Tomorrow there will be nothing again. We must just stay in the saddle."

"That is something, Daha-hen . . . to keep riding." The boy rode silently for a few minutes. "What then?"

"Then we will find the horses and take them back," the warrior said. He was silent for a few minutes. "Are you afraid of the white men and their guns?"

"I do not think so," the boy answered. "All my life people have been throwing things at me . . . Indians and white men." He rode quietly. "But we do not have many cartridges."

The warrior looked at the boy. "I have one cartridge. You have six. You have more cartridges than I have. Whatever we have will be enough because it is what we have. This way we will be economical. We will make each shot effective rather than firing promiscuously. A battle is not just bullets and guns. The brain must also work."

The boy's mouth drew to one side. "I am not very smart," he said.

Daha-hen considered the sky above them. "Do you know the Great White Man?"

"Is it the moon?" asked the boy.

Daha-hen nodded. "And the Great Kiowa?"

The boy pointed to a group of stars, including the Pleiades. Again Daha-hen nodded at the boy's answer. "Some say that group is the seven Kiowa sisters and their brother. But other men see the Great Kiowa there."

Thomas knew he should drop back in line behind Daha-hen, but he could not. He needed to be near someone and not alone with his fears and bad dreams. Daha-hen did not rebuke him.

"It is lonely here," the boy observed. "I hear my own thoughts too loudly."

"You will learn to keep company with even your most dreaded thoughts," the man said. "They are faithful and never leave you out here. That is why so many men could not ride alone or with just a few men. They must have a great company about to protect them from their own thoughts. But, finally, you must either accept the thoughts or drive them away."

"Do you ever doubt yourself, Daha-hen?" the boy asked.

"In fighting, no," the man said. "But I doubt many times my thoughts on men. There were men I misjudged . . . not fighting men, for I understood them. I knew who would fight and who would run, who to trust and who to watch. I even came to know who would die. But there were men I misjudged. I could not see them or their thoughts. And now those same men and their thoughts seem so clear to me. They ride beside me. But that is good. I can consider them."

"Who were those men?" the boy asked.

"Kicking Bird was one," said Daha-hen, shifting in the saddle and settling into the moonlight walk that would rest the ponies. "I did not like him. At first I thought he was a coward. But he was not a coward. He would fight. He could fight, too. He was a very smart man. When the People began to think he was a coward, afraid to go against the whites, he made a raid. I saw what he did. He did not look for women and children to kill. He took on the soldiers. It was a good fight. He came home then, and sat down just as before, content among the children and women, listening to the white men, taking their road. After that I thought he was a traitor, a betrayer of the People and their way. I did not respect him. I had contempt for him for a long time. But he saved my life. And I did not think to save his."

"Mamanti killed him with a curse," Thomas said.

"Did he? Tonight he is alive and riding beside me," Daha-hen said.

Thomas looked at Daha-hen. His copper face showed no tumult or fear. He was calm, matter-of-fact. The boy almost looked around him to see if, indeed, Kicking Bird rode on his other side. He wondered if he should be afraid and run away from this man and his thoughts. He searched his mind for some support.

Thomas remembered the words the People had said about this warrior — that he was peculiar. The words, coming from his mouth, were peculiar. The Kiowas did not speak of the dead or use their names, lest their spirits would come and haunt the speaker. It was bad medicine. And, then, the boy remembered. Daha-hen was the Man Without Medicine. He did not believe such things. He was not afraid of the spirits or his own thoughts. The boy sat back.

"Pacer's camp was full of dogs," Daha-hen spoke his thoughts to the moonlight. "A man could not walk among

133

them without a stick. Pacer . . . he was a Kiowa-Apache chief, you know . . . could not bear to kill them, eat them, so there were many dogs, always barking, always fighting. Kicking Bird's camp was full of children. They ran out to him whenever he came home. His own children, except for one daughter, and his beloved wife were dead then, but everyone's children ran to him. He gathered them to him like sweet-smelling flowers. He took them on his lap and told them stories even when enemies . . . Kiowas and white men . . . were in his camp."

Chapter Seventeen

"He was very large and powerful, that Great Kiowa."
Kicking Bird wrapped his arms around the child he
held. "He could step over rivers. He made everything
. . . this Kiowa land full of mountains and plains and
rivers, the great herds of buffaloes, and all the other
animals, little and big. He did not make cows, probably
not sheep, except on the mountains." He said this em-
phatically, teasing the children with his words. Their
black eyes focused on Kicking Bird's face. One of the
small boys who stood beside him put his arm around
the man's shoulders.

"One day, when he was walking about in the Far West,
the Great Kiowa found a very large hollow log. He feinted
at it three times with his spear. And the fourth time he
struck it. Out came the Kiowa people . . . grown men
and women.

"They ran away. He called them back. 'I am your father,'
he said. 'I made you. You are my children.'

"He looked at them very closely. They were not formed
quite right. Something was on their foreheads that should
have been on their arms or legs.
Kicking Bird turned the child on his lap to him and
looked closely. The child giggled and squirmed. The chief
found an imaginary part protruding from its forehead and
popped it off with a click from his tongue. He then stuck

it thoughtfully on the child's leg, studied it, and smoothed it down.

"Better," he said, as had the Great Kiowa, then returned to his tale.

"The Great Kiowa struck the log again. Grown men and women came out. They ran away. He brought them back. 'I am your father,' he said. 'I made you. You are my children.' This time there was nothing wrong with them, so he let them go.

"When the Great Kiowa struck the log the third time, grown-up men and women came out and . . . children. And the Great Kiowa knew they had been creating behind his back, so he refused to make any more. 'I will make no more Kiowas,' he said angrily. 'So it is entirely up to you.' And he left it to them." The children giggled.

"He gave every man a bow and every woman a tool to dress buffalo hides. He taught them to use the tools. He also taught the women to make clothes and teepees. When he finished, he said: 'I give you, Kiowas, all this country to travel about in and all the animals for food, clothing, and lodges.'

"Then the Great Kiowa went away toward the rising sun until he came to a great water. There he met for the first time the Great White Man. The Great White Man rode a very fine horse and wore beautiful clothes.

"The Great Kiowa said to the Great White Man: 'This is my country. I have made a people to live in it. These people are my children. I have given this country to them. It is theirs.'

"The Great White Man said back to him: 'You have done well. It is a good country. I myself have many children who live across the water in a country I have made and given to them. I have also given them books . . . and taught them to make fine clothes like I am wearing . . . and to build strong houses to live in. I have taught them to make the ground produce food for their sustenance.'

"The Great Kiowa went away thoughtfully and returned to his children. He told them of the Great White Man and his children. 'You are my children,' he said to them. 'I have made this country for you.' "

Kicking Bird looked up from the children around him to the three white men who sat around his fire. There was no threat in his eyes or voice as he continued.

"The Great Kiowa told his children: 'The Great White Man has made a country for his children beyond the great water. They should stay there. But, I do not think they will stay there. If they come to the country I have made for you. . . .' "

Kicking Bird stopped his telling and nodded to one of the older boys who continued: " '. . . You must fight them and never make peace with them. There are many more of the Great White Man's children than there are of you. But you will always be a people. You will continue forever.' "

"After a while," Kicking Bird, picking up the story again, drew the boy to him by his shoulders, "after a while the Great Kiowa and the Great White Man went up among the stars to look at what they had done and watch over their works. The Great White Man became the moon. And the Great Kiowa became a cluster of stars."

Kicking Bird bowed his head for a few moments, then raised it. "Take the children outside," he said, releasing the boy. "Show the children the Great White Man and the Great Kiowa together in the sky." The children scuttled over Kicking Bird and each other and went outside into

137

the prairie night with its dazzling dome of stars.

"That's quite a good story," said the white agent.

"And what do you think of it, Thomas Battey?" asked Kicking Bird of the man at his side.

"I have never heard it before," answered the Quaker whose steel-rimmed spectacles concealed soft gray eyes. "But it is not, I think, a friendly story for children."

Kicking Bird pulled his crossed legs toward him and took his pipe. "It is an old story, Thomas, told around many fires for many generations of Kiowa children. As you have seen, the older ones already know the ending." He drew on the pipe. "I think the Great Kiowa was wrong when he told his children to fight the white people and never to make peace. This tradition has been put into the minds of our children since infancy. It is always told the same way. The children grow up with it, and it is hard to wipe it from their minds. They are raised with a secret enmity toward the white people."

Kicking Bird looked at the other men around his fire, wise men of the Kiowa nation, including them in his words to the whites. "In this camp and many others we now receive rations and annuities from the white men. You are teaching our children about the white man's books. You are caring for us. Our hearts warm toward you. If it were not for this old story, which was planted in our hearts as children, the Kiowas would long ago have been friends with the whites.

"My wife, who has now gone ahead to our People, was a good and gentle woman. She received many kindnesses and favors from the agents and other white people. She loved you and always spoke of her friendship for the white people."

"All of us, who knew Ap-pean-ha, thought well of her

138

and only returned her friendship," said Agent Haworth.

Kicking Bird looked about his lodge at the Kiowa men. Most were men of his band, aware of his thoughts and ways. A few like Daha-hen were not. He had come to draw the young men away into raiding against the Texans. When Kicking Bird spoke, his words were for Daha-hen as well as for the white men.

"I have told my people that I have taken a new road. If my young men go into Texas to steal and murder, I will throw them away. If there are those who still will follow me, I will take them and go to the agency and settle down with the whites. This is my decision. I will live in peace. I now leave each man to the consequences of his choice."

Daha-hen's eyes burned brightly. "The white men hold our chiefs as prisoners in Texas. Their surveyors are now putting stakes into our land. Their hunters are killing our buffalo. You will sit down and sup with our destroyers, Kicking Bird. I will lead your young men who still wish to be Kiowas against their enemies. These white men will not hold me hostage on my own land."

Kicking Bird gazed at the warrior across the fire. "I have spoken my decision. I now leave each man to the consequences of his choice."

"Tell me, Thomassey," said Daha-hen to the boy who rode beside him, "what did the Great Kiowa say to his children about the Great White Man's children?"

"He said: 'You must fight them and never make peace with them.' "

"That is what I thought," said Daha-hen.

Chapter Eighteen

Broken Stick did not like the morning any better than the long night in the saddle. He was stiff and his muscles ached. *"Dapom!"* he spit out as he saw Thomas ahead, riding behind Daha-hen. "Elk, that *dapom* has taken your place."

Elk turned back to him. "Be quiet, Broken Stick. You are a rattling gourd. All night you have complained and said nothing that is useful."

Broken Stick shrugged. "I don't have to say anything useful. Anyone can see the *dapom* has taken your place."

"Try to be pleasant," Gnat Catcher said. "Everyone is tired. You are only making things worse with your words."

"Who made you chief, little Gnat Catcher?" asked Broken Stick. "When will that old man turn back? Even now I doubt that I will ever father children. Enough is enough."

"Shut up," said Elk. "We will ride until my uncle says we have gone far enough."

"Your uncle is crazy," said Broken Stick in a loud, taunting whisper. "Everyone knows he is crazy."

Elk rode on without answering. Broken Stick became quiet. His horse stumbled in the rocks. "Damned old man," he said. "I will not ruin my fine horse for a crazy old man. This is a fine buffalo pony."

"A buffalo pony," Gnat Catcher said to himself. "A buffalo pony holds the buffalo and only turns away at the twang of the bow string. Your horse turns away at a fart."

"What did you say, little Gnat Catcher?" asked Broken Stick.

"I said we must not lose heart," he answered.

The prairie shimmered before the riders. Thomas had slept little, but he did not feel tired. He bit off a piece of jerked meat. As he chewed, he relaxed his legs on the little horse and let it move him rhythmically with its stride. When he had eaten his breakfast, he sipped water from the gourd on his saddle, and put it away.

As he rode, the boy thought about Daha-hen's words from the night before. Broken Stick had said he was crazy. He said everybody knew Daha-hen was crazy. Thomas did not know. He wondered if the man was crazy. He was not sure about that.

Thomas was certain that Daha-hen would not turn back, and that he would get his horses with or without the boys' help. He was sure that Daha-hen knew just where he was going and just what he would do. He was also sure that, if they all died as they rode, Daha-hen would not turn back until he had done what he had set out to do.

Thomas realized that Daha-hen did not need them. He was complete and perfect without the boys. He was allowing them to ride with him, educating them in the lost ways of the People.

"Ahe," the boy said aloud in realization.

All his life Thomas had said to himself in his hurt, when they drove him away, that he did not need anyone. But he had known in his heart that he did. He had

141

not only needed, he had wanted. His heart was hungry for other beings of his kind. But they did not want him. They did not want Daha-hen, either. And he did not care. He was not made great or small by their wanting. He did not need such men or their medicine. Daha-hen was himself — a man, as the Great Kiowa had made him.

Throughout the morning Thomas thought and watched the land, shimmering in the growing heat. Ahead just a short distance was a lake. There were islands, tree-covered islands, in the lake. The trees swayed back and forth in the prairie wind that kissed his face. As the riders drew near, the lake gradually disappeared. Then Thomas saw it farther on. The lake and trees moved as always before them, drawing near, then pulling away. Thomas glanced to his right and saw the river that fed the lake a long way off. It was a long, winding river, fringed with timber. The banks were clearly visible to the boy. The river flowed now ahead of them, and then to the left and down into what had become a great sea. Upon the shores of the shimmering sea waves rolled and broke in foaming surges. Down the shore a grove of trees offered blissful shade from the sun.

As he rode, Thomas watched river and sea and grove disappear as in a dream, swallowed by the atmosphere. It was illusion, he knew. *Many thing were illusions,* he thought.

"We will rest the horses now," Daha-hen stated.

Thomas awoke quickly from his reverie. He saw that the sun had passed its zenith. The morning had slipped away. The land had changed as he had watched the mirages.

Daha-hen had brought the young men and their horses

to water. He sat in the stream on his pony as the animal drank from the water about its chest. With one hand he scooped water and brought it to his mouth. When he had drunk, he opened his hand and wiped the wetness over his face.

"We will rest now and let the horses graze," he said.

The older boys pushed passed Thomas into the water. They let their thirsty horses drink in the midst of the stream. Broken Stick stood on his horse's back and stripped off his shoes, shirt, and trousers. When he was naked, he dove into the stream. Elk and Gnat Catcher were soon beside him. Their clothes and weapons were left tied to their saddles on the loose ponies.

Thomas did not join them. He stopped on the bank and let the pony nuzzle the water. Squatting beside it, he drank from his hand. He rubbed his eyes and face as he had seen Daha-hen do. He took a rag from his pocket and wet it. He wrung it out over his head until the short black hair was wet, then tied it about his neck.

Daha-hen rode out of the water onto the far bank. The boys' horses wandered after his horse, still blowing the water and stamping. The warrior dropped to the ground and loosened his saddle. He took his horse up into the grass to graze, slipped the bridle, and fastened the hobbles about its feet. When he had looked about, Daha-hen lay down in the shade of the trees.

Thomas watched the splashing boys. A smile, the harbinger of an idea, dawned on his face. Very slowly he mounted his pony and rode into the water. The other boys ignored him at first, then slapped the water, shooting it at him. He rode on. When he reached the other side, Elk and the others were dunking each other.

Thomas quietly gathered their ponies' reins and led

them up out of the water into the grass beside Daha-hen's hobbled horse. But he did not stop. He kept riding, leading the horses slowly away and out of sight.

The young men splashed and laughed. Daha-hen slept. After a while Thomas returned without the horses. He sat on his grazing pony, watching the water fight.

Broken Stick looked up at him with water streaming from his long hair. He put his hands on his naked hips. "Hey, *dapom*," he shouted, "I once had two quarters so I had sex with your mother. So did my brother and uncle."

The other boys laughed and flipped backwards into the water. Thomas stiffened. His right fist tightened against his thigh. Under the tree Daha-hen rose to an elbow. The boy looked down, coughed, moved his jaw slowly from side to side.

"Where is your horse, great stallion of the Kiowas?" he asked, clearing his tight throat.

"He has taken the horses," Elk said, spitting and rising from the water.

"And our clothes," said Gnat Catcher flatly.

"Damn him." Broken Stick spoke quietly to the others. "This time I will make him sorry. It may be that this time I will kill him."

"How?" asked Gnat Catcher. "Your weapons are on your horse."

"Come down here now, *dapom*," Broken Stick ordered, ignoring Gnat Catcher's observation.

"Perhaps you should come up here," said Thomas. "There may be women about who will be impressed by your nakedness."

Gnat Catcher giggled, shoving Elk into Broken Stick's side. "Shut up," said Broken Stick. "You are as naked as I am." The other boys straightened slightly. "That *dapom* has taken a valuable horse that my father gave to me."

Broken Stick reached into the water and picked up a large smooth stone. Rising, he hurled it at Thomas, hitting him near the eye, knocking him backwards on his pony. Broken Stick ran from the water up the bank after Thomas Young Man.

Still holding his eye, Thomas whirled the pony away, back up into the grass. Broken Stick stooped and picked up a stick from the bank. He ran toward Thomas. He began to swing the club, hitting the little horse across the nose and head, again and again.

Thomas and the horse backed away, retreated. Broken Stick pursued, striking the horse again until the driftwood stick broke. Blood poured from the horse's nose.

"Where is my horse, you son of a bitch?" swore Broken Stick. "I said I want my horse now, or I'll kill this worthless rabbit you ride. It already bleeds like a pig." He laughed coarsely, turning his head slightly to catch the approval of his comrades.

Thomas shot from the horse, falling on the older boy. The two rolled about in the grass and rocks. Broken Stick pounded Thomas's side with his fist. The smaller boy coughed and dug in, ramming his shoulder into the other's stomach. Still grappling, the boys got to their feet.

The other boys came out of the water and walked toward Broken Stick and Thomas. Very quietly Daha-hen rose and put his hand on Elk's chest, stopping him and Gnat Catcher.

Grasping Thomas's cropped hair in his fist, Broken Stick struck the boy hard in the face — once, twice, and again. The boy became limp, a weight in his hand. Satisfied, he threw him back against the ground. Thomas lay still, on his back.

Broken Stick bent over him, pulled him up by the hair again. "Where's my horse, *dapom?*"

Thomas came around slowly with the shaking. The world swam before his eyes.

"Get my horse, chicken shit," said Broken Stick.

"Get it yourself," Thomas whispered hoarsely. He reached out for something, anything to hold him to the ground as Broken Stick lifted him, jerked him about like a doll by his hair. His hand found a piece of broken limb. Thomas quickly brought his knee up into Broken Stick's exposed crotch. As the bully grabbed himself and rolled away, Thomas skittered to his shaking legs and brought the wet limb down hard on the back of his head. Broken Stick fell onto his hands, then collapsed.

Thomas moved away and turned to the others with the weapon held ready in his hand. His black eyes spit all the anger of his years as a *dapom.*

"Come on," he said.

Elk and Gnat Catcher turned their backs to him and sat down. Thomas did not take his eyes off any of them. Very slowly, still holding the broken limb, he backed toward the pony. He caught the reins without looking. He quickly threw himself into the saddle. Safe on the pony he straightened.

"You will find your ponies as you walk home," Thomas said. Broken Stick moaned and raised himself, then dropped back onto his chest. Thomas continued: "I do not need fools. Fools like you would only get in the way and get us killed."

Daha-hen considered the bloody boy and his bloody

146

horse. He looked at Elk and Gnat Catcher, sitting naked with their elbows on their knees.

"Pick up your friend," Daha-hen said. "And start walking."

When the figures had become small against the horizon, Thomas went down to the water. Falling from the horse onto his shaking legs, he sank almost to the ground. He wet the rag from his neck and began to wipe the pony's bloody muzzle. He stroked the horse's head and spoke to it gently as he rewet the rag and washed the wounds.

"It is not much of a horse," said Daha-hen.

"It is my horse," flared Thomas. "It is my horse, and it depends on me. I will never let this horse down . . . never. I will always take care of this horse."

Daha-hen saw the boy's heart in his words. Thomas had been let down by everyone to whom he had belonged. In his child's heart he had determined never to do that to anything that belonged to him.

"But it has a noble heart," continued Daha-hen. "On the whole it performs much better than that fine buffalo pony."

"I have trained him," the boy said proudly, then added quietly, "but he was willing."

"You are like the old men about your horse," said Daha-hen. "A man knew better than to touch the old men's horses. To do so was to die without delay. A man's horse and dog were sacred. But that is forgotten." He watched the boy and the horse. "Thomassey, did you intend to run off the other boys?"

"I intended to play with their smugness, but it turned out well enough, running them away. They are grumblers. They would get us killed. They were too many for a miracle anyway." The boy began to wash his own wounds as the pony drank beside him.

"Miracle?"

"Old Gideon," answered Thomas. "Remember God told him to send off those that drank like dogs. Those Kiowas drank like dogs. More than that, they played water games and did not watch for the enemy."

"Thomassey, do you think medicine will fight for you if we have to fight?"

"No," the boy said, looking into his face. "God made me complete and whole. That is enough. I will do the fighting."

Daha-hen looked away. "No owl prophets for you, Thomassey?"

"I leave my fate with God," said Thomas Young Man. "You might as well know this, Daha-hen. I am a man who needs a God. As anyone can plainly see, my own power is small. I have taken the Methodist's God. My experience with Him has been good. He is not a bag of dog teeth or feathers that men can carry about, either. They say He has put his spirit in me now that I am a Christian. That is good because before my own spirit was very weak. Today I was not weak. I am thankful for that."

Daha-hen took Thomas's horse's nose in his hands. He gently stroked the wide forehead and lifted the nostrils up to study. "His nose will be sore. For a big boy that Broken Stick does not do much real damage." He reached for the bag at his belt and removed a piece of oily sheep's wool and smoothed it over the abrasions. "Or maybe your God keeps His eye on you and your horse, Thomassey. Right now I want you to go and lie down and sleep. I will hobble the horse to graze. We will ride on again when he has eaten and your legs stop shaking. Thomassey," he said as the boy moved haltingly toward the tree, "every man needs a god."

In the late afternoon the two Kiowas came to the top of a rise in the prairie. Before them lay the wide valley of the Canadian. Daha-hen sat silently for some moments, looking at the once-familiar terrain. Smoke rose from the chimney of a distant ranch house.

"Someone lives out here," the boy said.

"The Rancher lives here," Daha-hen said. "I came here two times . . . once to trade horses, once with other men to buy buffalo for the *Kado*."

"You went to the Sun Dance?" asked the boy.

"It is said that a warrior who does not attend the *Kado* will die," Daha-hen answered.

"So you went for the medicine, after all," said the boy.

"I went for the women," said Daha-hen. "They were very friendly at that time. And I went for my family and friends. It was a very pleasant time . . . good food, laughing, dancing." He nudged his pony off the hill toward the ranch house.

Chapter Nineteen

The ranch house was sturdy and comfortable, an organic construction of sod, wood, and stone, growing out of the land itself. Around it the few corrals, barns, and bunkhouse created a self-sufficient world where men could work the animals that were so much a part of their lives.

Old Tafoya saw the riders before they came off the hill. He threw the saddle he had repaired up on the corral rail and walked quickly back to the house. "*Señor*, there are two Indians coming in."

The Rancher looked up from the books spread on the kitchen table. His wife continued to lay dried apples in a bed of dough. "I'll be out in a minute," he said.

"Reckon what?" the woman said.

"We'll see." The Rancher stood up, stretched his powerful frame, and walked to the small window. He rested his hand on the sill. The riders were closer now. The man rubbed the sill thoughtfully. "This old place has seen some days, served us well. Forted up quick when we saw an Indian in the old days. Things have changed, Manda."

The Rancher took his hat from the elk-horn rack beside the door and went outside. He stood beside Tafoya with his hands on his hips, as the two Kiowas rode into the yard.

"Why, hell." Tafoya recognized one of the men. "Is that you, Daha-hen?"

"Tafoya?" Daha-hen stopped his horse before the man. "Has Quanah not yet killed you?"

"Not yet," said the old Comanchero. "Not yet by a damned sight."

"What brings you to our place?" the Rancher asked.

"We are going after the men who stole my horses," Daha-hen answered.

The Rancher considered the weary riders before him. Both were gaunt. Deep shadows lay beneath their eyes. They were clad in rags of white man's clothing. Only their moccasins and Daha-hen's hair and silver spoke of the old ways. The Rancher had fought the Indians as he had fought the droughts and the northers. It had been a good fight. For a time it could have gone either way. He believed his kind had prevailed in the end because they were just men.

Still, he thought, the Kiowas deserved better than they had gotten from Washington. What the hell did Washington know about the Kiowas or the men who'd fought them? Faceless beings in offices know nothing of the look in a man's eyes as he tries to kill you, or as he dies from your bullet. They can't see despair or read honor in a man. Paper robbers, that's what Washington was, a bunch of paper robbers who stole whatever a man had — hope, honor, anything — and never took a risk themselves.

"Can you rest and eat a spell?" signed the Rancher. "I'll check my men. Maybe they've seen something."

"Get down, then," Tafoya seconded his boss' words in Comanche.

Daha-hen stepped down. Thomas gratefully followed.

151

The men shook hands all around and followed the Rancher into the house. Inside, the woman had cleared away the table and set places for the man and boy. Hot dried-apple pies sat on the table; more cooked in the elegant iron stove hauled in from Kansas. She poured crockery mugs full of black coffee and put down plates of red beans and cornbread. The Indians did not acknowledge her but ate heartily from their plates. While they ate, she cut a pie and lifted out the slices onto smaller plates. The Rancher slid them across the table in front of the diners. The woman left, returned with more coffee, and poured some into Thomas's cup.

"Thank you, ma'am," the boy said.

"Why," she paused, then went on, "you are welcome, son." The woman continued to pour coffee into the other mugs but cast a glance at the Rancher.

"You speak English, son?" asked the Rancher.

"Yes, sir."

"What's the story here? What pulled you out from the reservation?" pursued the Rancher.

"A gambler came to Daha-hen's camp. He located the herds and came back after them with four other men. Daha-hen got a paper from Agent Hall so that we could go after them. We've been following them hard since he got back . . . that's two, no, three days ago."

The boy stopped to cut into the pie. He looked up at the woman who stood with arms folded over her apron, watching him eat. "You must be a Methodist, ma'am. Your food is so good."

The woman smiled at the boy's innocence. "Hunger adds taste to anything. But thank you. I don't hear many comments on the cooking around here. Them missionaries is doin' a fine job on you. Couldn't hurt anybody to have more manners."

The Rancher pulled out his pocketknife, intending to work a piece of wood he carried in his pocket. Then he changed his mind and rose. "While you finish up, I'll go see what the men might have seen when they've been out. Could be, they spotted your herd." He retrieved his hat and left.

"So how's civilization treating you?" Tafoya asked in Comanche.

"I do pretty good," said Daha-hen. "Got good horses, good grass."

"Ain't got them horses now, though," Tafoya observed.

"Maybe so." The Kiowa continued to eat. "But I will have them soon."

"You aim to fight them horse thieves?"

"Agent Hall said, if they shoot at me, I can defend myself." Daha-hen finished his meal and looked about for something to wash his hands in.

"Manda," Tafoya said to the woman. "You got a bowl of water over there. Daha-hen and the boy need to wash their hands off."

The woman set the bowl of water in front of the warrior. "White folks wash before they eat . . . Indian folks after. Strange happenings. Boy, what's your name?"

"I am called Thomassey . . . my name is Thomas Young Man. My father was an important warrior, but he was killed at Palo Duro Cañon."

Daha-hen looked at Tafoya who was studying his boots. "Tafoya knows Palo Duro," he said with a smile. The boy looked at the contemplative Comanchero, expecting further information.

"I'd as soon as not you didn't mention that," Tafoya said, without looking up. "That was a hard time. That

General Ranald Mackenzie was a hard man. I would never have told him where the cañon entrance was."

"But you did," said Daha-hen.

"Well, he hung me from a wagon tongue till I did, Daha-hen." The Mexican stood up and moved away.

"Quanah doesn't care. He still wants to kill you for betraying us." The Kiowa followed him to the chairs beside the empty fireplace. Thomas moved after the other men and sat on the cool hearthstones.

"I was bringing you guns and ammunition and trade goods when he caught me," Tafoya explained. "I never once offered him any information. But, when he saw the guns, he was one mad *gringo*. So he had the soldiers jerk me up, put a noose around my neck, and throw the rope over the wagon tongue. Still I said nothing. But, when they kicked the stool away, I was left dangling, barely able with my hands to keep the rope from strangling me." Tafoya pulled down his collar to show Daha-hen where the rope had scarred his throat. "And, my friend, you know I am not a brave, wild Kiowa. I am just a trader. That time I traded information for my life."

"Why are you not trading still?" asked Daha-hen.

"Well, when Mackenzie put you out of business, he put me out of business at the same time. Oh, I went back to New Mexico after he let me go, but I never could make a go of my business again. Something was missing."

"Your thievery," said Daha-hen. "No white man would pay you what you stole from the Indians."

"That may be," Tafoya agreed. "But you *hombres* were glad for the goods. Nobody else would take the risks and endure the hardships to deliver it to you. Hell, no-

154

body else could find the Valley of the Tongues. A man must be paid for his trouble. You'll have to admit I cheated you less than most. The guns I sold worked. The whiskey wouldn't burn a hole in a rock."

"That's true," agreed Daha-hen amicably. "Tafoya, why are you here with the Rancher? You are no cowboy."

"I went bust," the Mexican answered. "The *señor* found me sleeping behind the *cantina* under some boards. He said: 'You, Tafoya, come home with me. This ain't no place for a man your age.'

"I said: '*Señor*, I have traded for your stolen cattle for years. I am a great thief.'

"He said: 'That's right. Ain't nobody can keep as good a tally as you. You come on now and work for me.' So here I am, fat and happy." Tafoya paused. "You don't want to kill me like Quanah?"

Daha-hen shook his head. "No more killing for me, Tafoya. I did all I want. You are just a man. A man . . . even a Kiowa . . . will try to save himself."

"So it is true." The Comanchero smiled. "You did bring in Lone Wolf and Poor Buffalo to save your own hide. I heard Kicking Bird got you to do it, kept you out of prison for doing it, but I didn't believe it. 'Not Daha-hen,' I said. 'He hates white men more than any Indian I ever knew.' "

Thomas's ears grabbed the words. Was Daha-hen a traitor, a betrayer of other chiefs?

"I did not go to prison," Daha-hen said. "But I did not save my own life."

"Sure looks that way," observed the Comanchero.

"Looks are not always real," said Daha-hen. "Many times we see things on the plains that are not there. You know that."

155

Daha-hen fingered the stereopticon on the table beside a chair. He held it to his eyes and looked toward the light of the window. "Here, boy, look at this. There is a whole world out there you do not know about."

Thomas took the viewer. Before his eyes was a glowing three-dimensional picture of a town with tree-lined streets and big buildings.

Thomas Battey drew the stereoscopic viewer from his small bag of educational tools. It also included an "Alphabetical Object Teacher" and a kaleidoscope. But the day's lessons were over. His pupils were all warm beneath heavy buffalo robes. Most were slowly slipping into sleep. Now only the men remained around the late-evening fire. Winter was the tale-telling time of the Kiowas.

Battey had no great personal coup tales to tell, but he thought he could join the conviviality of the evening by bringing out the stereopticon. "Kicking Bird, here is something I have been showing the children. Perhaps you and your guests would like to see it?" The Quaker teacher slipped a card into the viewer. He held it up to his eyes toward the fire, checked it, then passed it to the chief.

Kicking Bird looked at the images which combined before his eyes. "I know that mountain. It is in the Far West. Many days' travel from here."

Beside him Setmaunte was eager to see the view that Kicking Bird so privately observed. When the chief started to hand it on, he took it quickly. Soon each man was struggling to get his turn and see what the others were talking about. They jostled and laughed, each snatching the object away from the previous viewer.

The stereopticon returned at last to Battey who removed the card and inserted a new one of Washington City. "This is the place where the government lives."

Kicking Bird held the viewer and studied the picture a long time. He handed it directly to Sun Boy, bypassing Setmaunte. "Is this the place you have told us about?"

Sun Boy took the viewer and looked at it quickly. "Ahe," he said. "That is Woosinton. I have walked just there, and I stood there under that small tree." He pointed, but the others could not see. "The streets are very hard in this area, covered over with small stones. Because of these streets their horses do not get muddy even when it rains. And their wagons can go in all kinds of weather without miring down."

Daha-hen took the viewer from him and pressed it to his eyes. He looked very closely at what he saw, moving nearer to the fire for more light.

"What you think now?" asked Sun Boy. "You think all lies now? You think all chiefs who have been to Woosinton fools now?"

Daha-hen passed the viewer on but said nothing. When Battey put in a new picture, he received it and studied it a long time before handing it on. Battey watched this militant chief's face. The Kiowa sat with his hand over his mouth, waiting to see more. His black eyes were alert and sharp, revealing the movement of thoughts in his mind. Like many of the Kiowas, Daha-hen felt the returning chiefs had been blinded or deceived in some way by the white men. What they spoke of could not be true. But, like the other Kiowas, Daha-hen also thought it was impossible to make an imaginary picture. A picture was proof of the existence of the original.

Battey replaced the picture with a view of the parade

157

of the Grand Army of the Republic. Soldiers stretched from the foreground to the horizon in immaculate uniforms and perfect order. Daha-hen received it. "Ahe!" a small gasp escaped his throat. He covered his mouth again and let the viewer pass. Battey kept replacing the pictures after the Kiowas had seen them. There were pictures of great bridges and railroad engines and harbors and ships and railway yards and fortifications with heavy cannons. Ladies with parasols strolled the streets of the spa town of Saratoga, New York. An interior of the hotel showed the dining room with many tables and diners.

Battey kept watching Daha-hen. When the stereopticon passed to other men, he sat thoughtfully with his hand over his mouth. When Battey had finished with all the cards, he was ready to put the viewer away, but the Indians wanted to see them again. After a second round of viewing most were satisfied and ready for other amusement. But Daha-hen had to see them again and again. Battey finally set the box of cards beside him and let him change them himself.

At last Daha-hen removed two cards and lay them before him on the floor. "I have seen this mountain." He pointed to it. "I know it is a true picture. Now I see this picture." He pointed to the other. Battey thought it was of the victory parade. "This also must be true."

Sun Boy and Lone Wolf nodded. "It is true. We have seen these things and many more," said Lone Wolf. "There are many fine buildings there . . . as big as mountains. We have told you, and you did not believe us."

Daha-hen still looked at the cards before him. He suddenly picked up the viewer and cards and went outside where another fire burned and warriors sat together. Battey followed. Daha-hen began to show them the stereopticon pictures. "Look what a mighty people they are! We are fools, Quitan!" He moved to another man. "We don't know anything! We are just like wolves, running wild on the plains." The men agreed, but the thought had not changed them as it had changed Daha-hen.

Chapter Twenty

The Rancher closed the door when he returned and moved to his large chair before he spoke. Daha-hen quickly abandoned his reverie. "Couple of the men saw a herd of horses being pushed north toward the Canadian yesterday. The herd was unshod from their tracks. My men counted almost a hundred head of good stock . . . quite a few spotted ponies like the one you are riding."

"It is my herd, then," said Daha-hen. "They are not so far ahead now." He stood up. Thomas clamored to his moccasined feet. He carefully set the stereoscopic viewer and cards back on the table. Daha-hen observed: "Our stomachs are full, and our ponies are rested. We will go on now."

"Yes." The Rancher offered his hand. "I expect you can catch up with them tomorrow if you ride all night."

Daha-hen shook the big man's hand and Tafoya's. As he and Thomas walked to the door, the Rancher's wife handed the boy a napkin full of still-warm biscuits. "You be careful now," she said softly.

The boy nodded. "Thank you again, ma'am, for everything. Your prayers will be appreciated."

The woman brought her hands to her mouth as the two Indians mounted their ponies and trotted out of the yard and back onto the plains. "Why that child's a Christian," she said to the Rancher.

"Hmm." He heard her words but had his own thoughts. "Damn' no-'count outlanders and outlaws coming into Texas again and stirring things up just when we get 'em settled down pretty good. Reckon they never thought some broken-down reservation Indian would take out after 'em. Near as I can tell, Daha-hen rode a hundred and fifty miles to Anadarko and back, and he's come another hundred and thirty this far in less than four days. That's tenacity. By God, I hope he nails their white thievin' hides."

"Easy, *señor*," Tafoya counseled. "Even a thief must live. And remember, Daha-hen was himself one of the best thieves of them all. We were all afraid of him. No telling how many horses and cattle he took . . . or scalps."

The Rancher's wife shuddered. "Ain't that long ago, either," she said. "All them poor people forgot now. Us standin' here today worrying about what happens to two Kiowas. Why back then, two or three Kiowas was enough to make us fort up in fear. Tafoya, you go check and see if my chickens laid any more eggs."

The woman returned to her kitchen.

Tafoya looked at the Rancher. "The greatest thief of all the Kiowas now goes after the thieves that have taken his horses. And the greatest Comanchero of them all now steals eggs from chickens, *señor*. It is a fickle world."

Daha-hen led Thomas quickly to the trail of the outlaws. They trotted along easily.

"How'd you know right where to find it?" asked the boy.

161

"Because I have been this way myself. It is the smoothest, easiest way to move horses."

"Then why'd we stop at the ranch?" Thomas pursued.

"I like to stop at the ranch. The Rancher is a good white man, and his wife cooks well."

"Did you steal from him, Daha-hen?"

The man looked at the boy. "It was not stealing then, Thomassey. It was business. A Kiowa's business was to take horses and scalps from white men. I was good at my business. The Rancher kept some pretty good horses. His cows were easily driven over into New Mexico."

"Then you stole his horses and cattle, and you still ate his food today."

"Thomas Young Man, the Methodists have ruined you. In many ways I am a brother of that man. We know each other's ways. We rode over this land before other men knew it was to be desired. But I could easily say he stole my land and my freedom and not be wrong."

"He stole your land and your freedom because you stole his horses and cows and killed people." The boy looked searchingly at Daha-hen.

"Thomassey, they were already taking the land. What business had a white man in this country but to take hold of it? It is their nature to possess things. We just didn't know that, didn't stop them soon enough. No one had ever come to stay before. We foolishly considered them a convenience. They brought things we wanted to trade for. They had good horses that were easy to take. It was good to have someone to fight with. Then they became too many to handle, unmanageable like too many horses. And there was no one to make up a big party and go after them."

Daha-hen pulled his horse into a walk before he continued.

"I have not been in this country since the Wrinkled Hand Chase. That was when I really knew for sure that the white men would not be stopped by us. We could not fight them forever. There were many of them and few of us. A Quaker let me look at pictures, like those in the Rancher's stereoscopic viewer, and they showed me that they were a powerful people. Their ways were wondrous ways to me. I realized we were like wolves, running on the prairies, compared to them."

Thomas Young Man said: "My father was killed in the Wrinkled Hand Chase. It has always bothered me that I don't know why. Whenever I ask anyone, they say that the People just ran away and hid at Palo Duro Cañon, and the soldiers caught them. Some of them got killed, and some of them ran away farther onto the plains, and some of them had to go to prison. But I don't know more about it than that, Daha-hen."

"These white thieves are like children," Daha-hen observed, ignoring the boy. "They think no one will follow, so they don't even try to cover their trail or take a different one. We will find them." He paused, then added: "I do not know why your father died. But I will tell you of the death of Kicking Bird."

"It is said that Mamanti killed him with medicine or maybe with strychnine." The boy did not want to know about Kicking Bird but about his father.

"Oh, that was at the very end." Daha-hen saw something in the tracks again. "There is my piebald mare," he said, and then resumed. "The death of Kicking Bird began long before that. It was a slow death . . . almost five years of dying before he went to the place of Many Lodges."

"I do not want to hear this about Kicking Bird," the boy said. "I know how Kicking Bird died. I do not know how my own father died, or why. All my life I have wondered because his death made me a *dapom*."

"I do not know how your father died, Thomassey. If I tell you of the death of Kicking Bird, you may discover something about your father's death. But maybe not. You will have to find that out."

"Tell me, then, about Kicking Bird's death." Thomas resigned himself to the story and the long ride ahead.

"We were great, wild men in those fading days. There was little that was more glorious than we were. Horses, maybe. We rode this land as lords. It was ours as far as the eye could see and beyond. Everything that was in it was ours . . . except the white men. Changes were coming with the white men. Changes we did not see and then, when we saw them, we did not like them. But the end was not yet . . . it was only beginning.

"Satanta and Adoltay and Satank were arrested for their part in the Warren wagon train massacre . . . that's what the white men called it. A hundred men had gone out with Satanta. Satanta was very strong against the white men since the meeting on Medicine Lodge Creek. The white delegates had killed our buffalo on their way to the meeting. This was not right. They were our food. It was our land. Satanta told them that. He also said then that Kiowas could not live confined, but they would not listen to him. Afterwards they expected us to live on a reservation and not go into Texas. And they sent the buffalo hunters down on us and the surveyors. It was pretty clear to everyone that the Indians were going to end up without any food and very little land.

"So Satanta thought he would get the white man's attention. He would hit the soldiers and their suppliers and the buffalo hunters and the surveyors until the white man listened. He would have a big success with many braves. But this was not to be.

"I was there. I saw it. We listened to Satanta. We went out. Mamanti made his talk with the owl. He told Satanta not to hit the first group that came by, but to wait for the second. The first group included the big general, Sherman. We did not get him. I have always regretted that. We killed seven *kota-dalhop* . . . freighters . . . instead. Some others got away and told Sherman and Mackenzie at Fort Richardson. That put the soldiers on our trail, but it had washed away in the rain storm, so they could not track us back to the Fort Sill reserve. But the old Quaker, Agent Lawrie Tatum, he knew Satanta had been gone. When Satanta came in, he asked him straight if he had done the killing.

"Satanta puffed up. The great orator said he, Satanta, had led the killing raid. Tatum . . . we called him Stone Head because he had no hair and because he could be very hardheaded . . . went to Sherman himself who was at the fort. Satanta followed him to Grierson's porch. He boasted that he had led the raid and that Adoltay, Satank, Eagle Heart, and myself had also shared the leadership.

"Sherman arrested Satanta on the porch and sent men to get the rest of the leaders. They summoned Satank, and the old man came. He did not care if he died. He was still leading his son's bones when he came in. Adoltay was at Shirley's store. He dove through a window, but they caught him anyway. Eagle Heart saw the sol-

165

diers coming and got away. I was not there. After the raid I had become disgusted with the Kiowas and went to visit my friends, the Comanches.

"Sherman decided to turn the chiefs over to the Texans at Fort Richardson for a trial. A trial is where many white men agree together what should be done with another man who has offended them. Kiowa people do not have such things. If a man kills another Kiowa, we know, and we leave him alone. We do not try to figure out whether he did it the way white people do. He does not deny the killing. We all know he has done it. The only time I know of the People getting together against someone was over a sorcerer once. He was causing everyone a lot of grief. He had to be rubbed out.

"They put the men in wagons to take them there. Satank pointed to a tree and told the others he would not pass it alive. He sang his death song. . . ."

"Coughed up a knife by his medicine power," added Thomas.

"Caddo George Washington told me he gave the old man the knife as he was leaving, but you can believe what you wish, Thomassey. He stabbed his guard in the leg and took his rifle to fire on the others. The rifle jammed. Looks like his medicine could have done better than that. But they killed him while he tried to get it to work."

"Many shots were required to kill him," Thomas put in from his limited knowledge.

"Two shots, that was all. The rest is exaggeration," said Daha-hen. "He fell off the wagon, and they left him there and went on. His second son came and got the body and buried it together with his brother's bones. Satank was satisfied then.

"In Texas there was a trial. The Texans found at the trial that Satanta and Adoltay were guilty of the murder of the teamsters. They were to be hanged, but the governor of Texas put them in prison instead. This was the beginning of much dissatisfaction and trouble."

"What does this have to do with the death of Kicking Bird?" asked the boy.

Daha-hen rode on in silence, checking the trail. Then he spoke again. "You will see in time. If the Kiowas quit raiding and brought in their captives, they could get their chiefs back. We did not raid any more that summer or winter. But we thought about what was happening.

"Some of us did not like this. We talked about it with our friends, the Comanches. Many Comanches remembered the Council House fight in Texas. The Texans had tried to hold their chiefs then for the return of their captives. There was a great fight. Some women and children were held. The Comanches staked their white captives to the ground and burned them alive. They were not interested in hostages. They would not be compelled to do what they would not do by choice.

"White Horse and I were like the Comanches. By spring we had decided to fight. There were only a handful of us and White Horse's woman. We went to Texas with the Comanches. Between El Paso and San Antonio we found an unescorted contractor's wagon train. The *kotadalhop* were Mexicans. We wiped them out, seventeen killed. We made sure the white men would remember what we had done."

"How?" asked Thomas.

"We burned eight of them to cinders on the wagon wheels. We also left one woman alive to tell of the deaths of her husband and baby. I do not remember who scalped

167

the baby." Daha-hen spoke without emotion. "We were very hard men. With that attack we had shown our contempt for the white man's bargain, so we came back home.

"But White Horse's brother, Kompaite, had been killed by soldiers near Fort Belknap while we had been away. His death had to be avenged. In June White Horse and I and a few others hit a place on the Clear Fork of the Brazos below Fort Griffin. This I have learned was called the Abel Lee place. We killed a man reading a paper on the porch, a woman in the house, and a big girl in the yard. We were very angry so we cut them up badly. We took three children captive.

"While we were raiding, the white men were also busy. But we did not know it then. Mackenzie . . . some called him No Index Finger or Bad Hand . . . went up onto the Staked Plains with soldiers for the first time. They had caught a Mexican who worked for the Comancheros."

"Was that Tafoya?" inquired Thomas.

"No. Tafoya came later. This was just a herd boy. He showed Mackenzie the trail to Puerto de Luna where we took the cattle we stole. He took the soldiers into the Valley of Tears and the Valley of Tongues."

"Why were those valleys given such names?" asked the boy.

"Do you know nothing of the People, Thomassey? The Valley of Tears was called that because it was there that the captives were separated. There was always much crying there, when women were taken from their children. The Valley of Tongues was called that because traders who spoke many languages or tongues came there to trade. That summer the white men found out

168

where there was grass and water on the *llano*. By the end of summer Bad Hand knew all our places of dealing with the Comancheros. It was the white man's first success in our country. They had found the door to our secret places.

"Our raids in Texas had gotten much attention. Everyone knew about them. There was a lot of raiding going on around the agency, too. Old Lawrie Tatum withheld rations until the Lee children we had taken were returned. Everyone was worried that war was coming. The Civilized Tribes wanted to talk with the Indians who had not yet taken the white man's road. They called a council to meet at old Fort Cobb at the end of July in the white man's year of Eighteen Seventy-two."

Chapter Twenty-One

"Where is Tatum, Lawrie Tatum?" shouted White Horse, the round-faced, pockmarked war chief, as he dropped from his horse in front of the interpreter, Horace Jones.

"He has gone home because you Kiowas and Comanches are so late in coming to Fort Cobb. His wife is ill," answered Horace Jones without a blink.

"I came here just to kill him," growled the Kiowa raider. "He is starving the women and children to get back captives. I will not put up with this. But now Tatum is gone, and you . . ." — he brushed his hand across the interpreter's shoulder — "you are not worth killing. I will let you off. You are not of sufficient importance."

"Sit down," said Kicking Bird to the blustering warrior as he walked past him into the shade. "We have come here to talk, not to fight. Let us hear what these Indians and this man, Beede, have to say." Kicking Bird resumed his seat in the council circle.

Cyrus Beede cleared his throat. "Your friends, the Wichitas and Caddoes, have called this talk, and we have thought it a good idea. This summer there has been much raiding. Things are very dangerous. Washington is becoming angry. We must stop this before his anger overflows."

The Kiowas and Comanches began to grumble as the chief clerk of the Superintendent of Indian Agencies spoke.

Lone Wolf stood up. "I am the head chief of the Kiowas. I speak for the Kiowas. This is what I have to say for the Kiowas. We do not accept this threat from Woosinton. You must remove Fort Sill and all these soldiers from our land. Our reservation must be extended from the Missouri on the north to the Rio Grande on the south. We have no intention of talking peace with you or anyone else until Satanta is returned to us unharmed. We will not promise to quit raiding in Texas as long as you hold our chiefs. Raiding these Texans is a Kiowa's legitimate occupation. That is what I have to say."

As Lone Wolf sat down, White Horse rose quickly to his feet. "Our young men will raid whenever it pleases them. I will not return the Lee children. Tatum cannot starve me into it. I am a man. I will find food for my people without this white man." White Horse pushed up the sleeve of his fringed shirt. He turned about, showing a deep healing wound on his forearm. "I have taken many wounds before this one. But this one I got at Howard Wells. I led that raid myself against those Mexican freighters. That kind of thing is what we will give the white man for his demands."

"This is not useful talk," said the Caddo chief. "Your words are full of anger and will draw anger from the white men. The Caddoes have taken the peace road, not in fear or under compulsion, but because it is a better road, a practical road.

"You Kiowas are not the only ones who have had trouble with the white men. The white men have also been our enemies. We could keep on being angry until all our people are dead. But this is not practical or reasonable. The Mexicans call the Comanches gente sin razón . . . people without reason. That may be true of the Comanches. It is

171

not true of the Caddoes. We are reasonable people. We do not like to have our houses burned or our children crying. We want to sit down in this place with our crops and our livestock and our children in peace. You war chiefs are making it hard on us and on your own people. Think about this. Go to your lodges and think about this. Tomorrow we will talk again."

The next day little had changed. Lone Wolf and White Horse still held a militant line. Neither the Caddoes nor the Wichitas nor the Quaker clerk had any effect on their anger. The war chiefs left the council as they had come, unchanged by the words of those who had hoped to prevent the war that was coming, defiant of the white men who thought they could make slaves of them by holding Satanta and Adoltay in the Huntsville Prison.

Horace Jones watched the men mount their horses and ride away. When he turned, Kicking Bird was by his side. "You tell Tatum that Kicking Bird does not agree with Lone Wolf and White Horse. I desire peace. I will do all that I can to get the children from White Horse. You tell Tatum that."

As quickly as he had come, Kicking Bird was gone. Jones rubbed his head and walked over to the table where Cyrus Beede sat with Major G. W. Schofield, acting commander of Fort Sill in Colonel Grierson's absence. Schofield made a complete report of the council and its confrontations to the Adjutant General.

In August Susanna and Milly Lee were brought to the Wichita Agency at Anadarko and turned over to Agent Richards. On September 30th six-year-old John Lee was delivered to Agent Tatum at Fort Sill. Kicking Bird had made his road and kept his promise.

Washington did not want a war. By September the government sent new peace emissaries to the wild tribes at Fort Sill. The plan was simple: bring the head chiefs to Washington, show them the might and power of the United States government. When they returned home, they would tell the others and perhaps discourage them from taking on so formidable a foe. Indians weren't fools. They were very selective in their opponents. The Army and the Texans knew they preferred lightly armed, solitary groups to fighting forces. A trip to Washington might turn the tide.

The Kiowas, Comanches, Cheyennes, and Arapahos came to the council along with the Caddoes and Wichitas. Unfortunately Daha-hen and the Quohadis remained out. The Kiowas refused to go to Washington. They distrusted the government. After all, two of their chiefs were already hostages.

A young officer, Captain Henry Alvord, left alone in his dealings with the Indians by the sudden death of his associate, Professor Edward Parrish of Philadelphia, offered the Kiowas a visit with Satanta and Adoltay. Washington had authorized him to promise the release of the chiefs, provided the Kiowas promised to observe their treaty obligations in the future. Many of the Quakers thought this was a despicable ploy since Washington did not actually have custody of the chiefs. They were in the hands of the Texans.

Alvord did not promise their release but said only that the Indians could see for themselves that the chiefs lived and were well treated. With that, after endless hours of negotiating, the Kiowas finally selected Lone Wolf, Sun Boy, Wolf-Lying-Down, and another man to be their delegates to Washington. But first they had to see the chiefs.

Alvord got Texas Reconstruction Governor Edward Davis to release Satanta and Adoltay into the Army's custody. The plan was to bring them from Huntsville to Dallas. Lieutenant Robert G. Carter, Fourth Cavalry, would pick them up there and escort them to Fort Sill for a visit with the delegate chiefs. At Denton Creek Carter was met by scout Jack Stilwell with a counter message from acting commander of the post, Major G. W. Schofield.

As the well-armed Kiowas had begun to gather at Fort Sill, Schofield saw the danger of a bloody fight when the chiefs arrived. With only five troops of cavalry on hand, he could not suppress a general uprising. Carter was to bring Satanta and Adoltay to Atoka. He was to hold the chiefs secretly there.

The delegate chiefs were taken by wagon to Atoka. There they boarded the train for St. Louis. Behind them a second train carried the prisoner chiefs. At the swank Everett House Hotel in St. Louis the Kiowas were reunited. It was obvious to the delegates that neither Satanta nor Adoltay had been abused at Huntsville. Satanta had been in a work gang that helped construct track for the railroad that carried him to Dallas. Adoltay had worked in the laundry. During his time in Huntsville Satanta had mellowed. He referred to himself as a Texan, as indeed he was. After a tour of the city, Satanta and Adoltay were returned to Huntsville. Lone Wolf, Sun Boy, and the other Kiowas went on to Washington.

Chapter Twenty-Two

Far to the west Colonel Ranald Mackenzie followed up his summer reconnaissance with the further implementation of Commanding General of the Department of Texas C. C. Augur's order to hit the Quohadi in their strongholds. About mid-afternoon on September 29th Mackenzie's Tonkawa scouts found a large Comanche village on McClellan Creek. The Indians were drying meat and making pemmican for their winter stores. They did not expect an attack.

Mackenzie attacked at a gallop. After a forty-minute fight around the lodges and in a nearby ravine, the Comanches broke and fled. Most warriors escaped. 120 women and children were captured. 1,200 horses were taken and 262 lodges were burned.

Mackenzie cautiously withdrew. That night, placing the women and children inside a corral of wagons, he lay down to sleep. The full force of the Comanche men hit the sleeping soldiers. With war whoops and cow bells and blankets waving, the Indians rode into the ponies, causing a general stampede. In the chaos some of the prisoners crawled through the wagons and escaped.

Mackenzie was angry, but wiser. He would not make the same mistake again. Never again would the Comanches get their horses back. At daylight he regrouped and pushed back toward Fort Griffin, and then on to

Fort Concho where the women and children would become negotiating pawns with the Quohadis.

The Kiowa delegates, meanwhile, had arrived in Washington. They spent most of October in the capital. They visited with the Commissioner of Indian Affairs and other prominent officials. The commissioner promised the Kiowas, if Governor Davis agreed, to return their chiefs in six months. The Kiowas, of course, had to promise good behavior. After a tour of several Eastern cities and points of interest, the chiefs returned in early November to Fort Sill.

Ten Bears, the eighty-year-old Comanche chief, was dying. At his great age the trip to Washington had been too much for him. Thomas Battey sat beside his bed. The other Indians had left the old man.

The Quaker watched the heavily wrinkled face of the once mighty chief. "Where are your people?" he asked softly, more for himself than for the dying man.

"It is the way of the plains to leave those who cannot live," said Kicking Bird behind him.

"Even his son won't come here," said Battey.

"Yes." Kicking Bird took a chair where he could see Battey's clear face. "Our ways are different, Thomas. The land and our traveling life make our ways different."

Battey turned to his friend. "You did not leave your wife when she was dying."

Kicking Bird looked down. "My wife was a good woman. She liked white people. Missus Tatum and others helped her when she lost her children. She is happy with her children now. I only have one child with me still. She is lonely and grieves for her mother. I have told her that her mother had to take care of her other children and

176

that I will take care of her. My other wife is good to the child. It may be that she will soon give my daughter a brother to take away her grief.

"I have found that when someone dies, someone will soon be born. I think it is like that with ideas or ways, too. When an old way is dying, a new way is being born. Do you have children, Thomas?" Kicking Bird's face was sad. The corners of his mouth pulled down into his characteristic expression.

"Yes," answered the Quaker. "I had three children. Before I came here, two of them and their mother died. I remarried. My wife now cares for my daughter with her own son. So I now have children again. I miss them, but my work is here."

"We are much alike, Thomas. I, too, have a daughter remaining. It is good to have children. A lodge should have many children and old people. A people cannot survive without children. Without old people there is no one to tell of the greatness of the past and give courage for the future. But children and old people cannot survive fighting and running. If the Kiowas are to continue as a people, the fighting must stop."

Kicking Bird stood up.

"You must come soon, Thomas, to my camp and begin to teach my children as you taught the Caddo children, as my wife wanted. I have asked you before. I will come and get you when you are ready. I will take care of you."

Kicking Bird left the Quaker beside the dying chief.

Thomas wet a cloth and placed it on the old man's forehead. "And what do you think in your great wisdom, old one? Can Kicking Bird save his children, his people? Is a new way being born for the Kiowas?"

Chapter Twenty-Three

"After the Quohadi women and children were taken to Fort Concho," Daha-hen continued his story to Thomas, "the Comanches were not so contemptuous. They missed their children and women. They came to Fort Sill for the first time. I came along, too. My family was camped near Kicking Bird's people. Kicking Bird had taken the peace road.

"Horseback had come back from Woosinton and had also taken the peace road. He went about, getting captive children from the Indian people . . . mostly boys that had not been adopted. He turned them over to Tatum. Five of his family members were returned to him from Fort Concho. One died on the road home. He and his women traveled around among the bands and told us that they had been well treated. We were glad to hear that.

"The Quaker was always going about with Kicking Bird. He drew pictures for the children and used them to teach the children about the scratches white men make to talk to other white men. He had a bag with several interesting things in it. That's where I saw the stereoscopic viewer for the first time. It made me see the white men differently. Lone Wolf and Sun Boy and Horseback and all the others had spoken of the things I saw. But now I saw them myself.

"The Comanche women's stories showed the white man to me in a different way also. Lone Wolf and the others said that Satanta and Adoltay were well treated in their captivity. They told us that the white men would release our chiefs in the spring. These things caused me to begin to think differently about the white men, about the peace road. I sometimes listened to Kicking Bird.

"That winter I was in and out of the camps, although I did not come to the agency. I stayed in the lodges and thought about what I had seen and heard. When spring came, I had made up my mind. I would not go out raiding on the Texans. I would watch my horses and be with my father and mother and the people of our band. I could have used another herd boy, too. But I did not go out to get a captive. I waited to see if the white men would keep their promise to return Satanta.

"The People were very quarrelsome among themselves that year. Among the Comanches a young man had killed his father and ran off to raid in Texas. Four other boys and two girls went with him. The Comanches reported this so that the government would not hold it against them and would still release their women. But these young raiders became important later on.

"Our chiefs did not come back in the spring. In June, when we went to the *Kado*, we still did not have our chiefs. The quarreling among us was getting out of hand. Black Bull lusted after Appearing Wolf's young wife. She was willing. So he stole her. Appearing Wolf killed six . . . no seven . . . of Black Bull's horses. He took several more really good ones for himself. Black Bull took all this with resignation. He knew that it was the husband's right to save face. Still Appearing Wolf was not appeased. His anger was eminent because he had really wanted

179

this woman. He said he was going to kill the woman and Black Bull. This was too much. The Dog Soldiers had a talk with him, and he changed his mind.

"Battey, the Quaker, was with Kicking Bird. Kicking Bird brought him to our council. The Cheyennes and Arapahos were taunting us, saying our chiefs had not been sent home even though we had not joined them in the raids in the spring. Battey told us that our chiefs were being held because some Indians we did not know . . . had never heard of . . . Modocs . . . had killed a white general and a Methodist preacher. He said there was a bad feeling among the whites towards Indians. If Woosinton let our Indians go, the other white people would be angry.

"Battey said he had written a letter for us. In it he had told the good things that we had done. He told Woosinton that we had not gone out raiding even though the Cheyennes had come around tempting us. He said that the Kiowas had intercepted parties of their own young men and others and held them.

The Cheyenne Dog Soldiers in Kicking Bird's teepee came on business. Kicking Bird called in the other chiefs to listen to them.

"We are going to begin raiding soon," their spokesman said. "We would like the company of our Kiowa brothers. We know that the threats from Woosinton will not intimidate you. You will not grovel like cowards to get your chiefs back. You will fight like men. I see Daha-hen sitting at this fire. I know that this Kiowa will never become a coward because of threats."

Daha-hen rubbed his eyelid with the finger of one hand. "Listen to me. You do not need to flatter me or try to draw me into your raid by implying I will not fight. It pleases me to sit down here among my people and watch what will happen about the chiefs. The only one I will fight now will be a lying, deceitful Cheyenne. I will take pleasure in cutting out your tongue and letting it pulse here on the floor before you."

"The Kiowas will talk among ourselves about what we will do," said Lone Wolf. "When we have decided, we will tell you."

The Cheyenne left Kicking Bird's teepee and went toward the fire that burned outside. He talked with the other men of his party as the Kiowas made their decision. The fire had burned low, and the Cheyennes had rolled themselves into their blankets to sleep, before the Kiowa chiefs emerged and went to their own lodges.

In the morning Battey washed his face and shaved in the small looking glass he carried in his gear and kept in the teepee he used. When he had put on his spectacles and read from his battered Bible, he sat quietly listening to the spirit that talked to those of his faith. Doeskin came into his lodge and stirred the coals of his fire. She mixed flour and water, rolled the pieces into balls, and patted them into rough biscuit shapes. She smiled at Battey as he came to the fire.

"Doeskin, you are a good cook," said the Quaker. "You are very thoughtful of my stomach."

The woman laid the biscuits on the forks of small branches that she kept to cook Battey's food. "Go out and see the Cheyennes who have come to get men to go with them into Texas."

The Quaker gently lifted the teepee door and walked out into the early spring morning. The Cheyennes were still rolled in their blankets, but some were cooking. Across

the village Battey heard the dogs start up. In a few min
utes Lone Wolf and the other chiefs entered the opening
where the fire burned. He waited for the women to serve
the visitors.

When the eating was done, Lone Wolf spoke. "You
Cheyennes have come to our camps to get young men
to go with you to Texas. We are against this. Last night
we decided to punish any Kiowa soldier who goes with
you or tries to go with you. We will kill his ponies and
burn his lodge. We will not allow you to pass through
us on our way to Texas."

Battey blinked. As silently as they had come in the
night, the Cheyennes gathered their gear, mounted their
ponies, and departed. Across the way Kicking Bird smiled
at him. Behind Kicking Bird, Battey saw Daha-hen.

It was three nights later when the Kiowas caught a
party of Cheyennes passing through their pony herds.
"You, Daha-hen," the young Dog Soldier called out. "Let
us pass. We are doing nothing that the Kiowas have not
always done. Nothing that you yourself have not done
many times. You are a renowned warrior because of what
you have done. Do you deny us the opportunity to rise
among our people, to strike against the venomous white
serpents?"

Daha-hen rode quietly around the group of young men
detained by his warriors. None of them was twenty years
old. All of them were eager as he had been to gain honor
to show bravery. "You, Eagle Plume. Here is what I say.
We will give you four talks. At the end of that time, if
you still insist on going into Texas, we will kill your horses
and break your weapons."

"You are becoming a woman like Kicking Bird," the
young man retorted.

"You are becoming a dead man even as your mouth continues to talk," said Daha-hen. The young man closed his mouth tightly.

Daha-hen bent and pulled a stem of grass from the trail. Then he spoke to Thomas Young Man. "Battey told us to wait until his letter had been received and a reply sent before accepting the invitation of the Cheyennes. Since the Comanche women had been released to their relatives at Fort Sill before he came out, he expected the clamor over the Modocs was dying down, and Woosinton would release our chiefs.

"The Sun Dance was very odd that summer. A medicine man called up a thunderstorm out of nowhere. Two Cheyenne women were struck by lightning and killed. Our women said it was because they had worn red blankets, and anyone knew that was a dangerous thing to do at a Sun Dance."

"Still it was a long time before Satanta and Adoltay came home. The trees were already dropping their leaves, and the wind had a winter-coming-soon sound. There was another big council at Fort Sill. The Texas governor was very hard with us. He was afraid of us and would not even come outside the fort to talk. We had to go inside. We hated that because our people had been arrested there. But Quakers talked to us. We knew they hated the fort almost as much as we did.

"The Texas governor was very arrogant. He said we must do several things. There were always more things we had to do . . . give up our weapons and horses, raise pigs, roll call. These were things some white man always wanted us to do. We also had to go with the Army and bring in anyone who was depredating in Texas.

183

Davis said we had to turn over the five young outlaws who had gone to Texas. They were led by the boy who had killed his father in the spring. This was very odd since they were Penateka Comanches, not Kiowas. We could not see what they had to do with our chiefs. The white men were jumbling us together again. Cheevers and Horseback and many other Comanches said they thought it was wrong to punish Indians who had lived peacefully because some other Indians had not.

"If we did not do what they wanted us to do, Satanta and Adoltay would be left in the guardhouse. When the Texans and the Army were pleased with our behavior, the chiefs would be released. But if we did anything wrong at all, they would be re-arrested and sent back to prison in Texas.

"We agreed to the conditions, if Satanta and Adoltay would be released at once without going back to the guardhouse. Davis would not do this. 'I will not change these conditions,' the governor said. The council closed."

Chapter Twenty-Four

Battey followed Kicking Bird beyond the fort. "You must not become discouraged."

"My heart is stone, Thomas," the Kiowa said. "There is no soft spot in it. I have taken the white man by the hand. I have thought he was my friend, but he is not my friend. Your government has deceived us. Woosinton is rotten. I have worked hard for peace. I have kept my young men from raiding. Woosinton has deceived me and broken his promises. There is nothing left for us but war. I know that war with Woosinton means the extinction of my people, but we had rather die than live like this."

"When the day's talk ended," Daha-hen told Thomas, "the Kiowas went back and spoke among themselves. They still had our chiefs at the fort. They had sat in council with us. If the white men would not listen to us, we decided that the next day at the council we would fight. Each man took his weapons under his blanket. The women and children were already pulling back, but a few stayed to make things look normal. They sat on horses ready to run away. We also had swift horses ready for our chiefs' getaway. Our men casually took positions around the fort from which they could easily shoot the governor and guard. When they tried to return our chiefs to the guardhouse, we would start the attack."

"Was it a big fight before the People ran away to Palo Duro?" Thomas asked.

"There was no fight. The governor turned the chiefs over to the Army and went back to Texas. Horseback and some other men went with the Army to find the five renegades but did not succeed. We went back to our camps and hunted buffalo. Satanta and Adoltay were with us. We forgot Woosinton and white men.

"When I came into camp with my ponies heavy with buffalo meat, Battey was waiting. Kicking Bird was coming in behind me but much more slowly. The next day it rained, and Kicking Bird did not arrive until evening.

"When we sat down in Kicking Bird's lodge, Battey had a letter for us from Agent Haworth. He said that Woosinton was not satisfied. He wanted the five renegade Comanches. Helping hunt for them was not enough. The Comanches had to find them and turn them over. Their annuities would be withheld until the men were turned over. They had just ten days. Haworth thought there would be trouble between the Comanches and the soldiers. He did not want the Kiowas to get into it."

Kicking Bird sat with his hand over his lips, listening to Thomas Battey read. Once the Quaker finished, Kicking Bird leaned forward, studying the fire. "When I was at the agency, they would not give me the annuities. If I go back there again, it may be the same."

"That was a packing error," said Battey. "The Kiowas' annuities were packed in with the Comanches'. Now they are separated."

"Last winter we were told to come in and sit down by the agent. We did. We got no robes to trade with, and it made us poor all the year. I want to know, if these

186

five chiefs camped here with me were to go in, would we get our goods?" Kicking Bird did not look at Battey.

"I do not know that," Battey answered. "But if you go in together, you can see that a fair distribution is made. One chief could not complain that he had gotten less than he should have. But that is not my doing, and I cannot answer for the agent."

"This country from the Arkansas to the Red River was given by Woosinton to his red children . . . the Kiowas, Comanches, Osages, Wichitas, Cheyennes, Arapahoes, Apaches, and Caddoes. It was a country of peace. I now see white men in it, making lines, setting up stones and sticks with marks on them. We do not know what it means, but are afraid it is not for our good.

"The commissioner by making this bad talk to the Comanches has set this country on fire. He has required a hard thing, which was not in the road our fathers traveled. It is a new road to us, and the Comanches cannot travel it. They cannot bring in five men. If they even attempt it, many women and children will be killed, and many men must die.

"This trouble the commissioner has made will not affect the Comanches alone. Look at Daha-hen. The Comanches are his brothers. A man will join his brothers, if he feels the demand made on them is impossible. This trouble will spread.

"I have taken the white people by the hand. They are my friends. The Comanches are my brothers. By and by, when I am riding on these prairies and see the bones of the Comanches or the skull of a white man lying on the ground, my heart will feel very sad. And I will say: 'Why is this?' And I will answer: 'It is because the Indian commissioner made a road the Indians could not travel.'

"If Woosinton would put his soldiers all along on the frontiers and kill every young man who goes across the line, we would cry for them. But it would be right. When they cross the line, they take the chances of war. A man's own people cannot turn him over to his enemies.

"The white man is strong, but he cannot destroy us all in one year. It will take him two or three, maybe four years. Then the world will turn to water, or burn up. It is our mother and cannot live when the Indians are all dead."

Battey could see that Kicking Bird was troubled. "Do you think that the Comanches did right to go raiding into Texas after promising the agent that they would do what he wanted if only they could have their women and children back. I heard them say that many times. They have gotten their women and children. And now they have gone back on the bad road, stealing horses, killing people.

"Washington has two kinds of children. He loves them both and does not want them to quarrel and kill each other. That is the road they used to travel. He is trying to make a good road for all his children . . . broad enough for them all . . . if they would not quarrel and fight. But Comanches go into Texas, steal horses, and kill people, and Texans come here and steal ponies. Washington steps between his children, takes both by the arm, holds them apart, and tells them they must stop quarreling. He says: 'I shall put my soldiers between you, then, if you fight, you fight me. Your quarreling must stop.'

"Now the Kiowas have nothing to do with this trouble. It is between Washington and the Comanches. Washington gave you back your chiefs. His heart is warm toward you. He has told his agent to give you your annuities. They are ready for you now. And I think you will not

188

be sorry if you go in and get them.

"It is because the agent loves you that he sent you this message." Thomas Battey's voice became quieter still. "It is because I love you that I brought it. I want you to listen to my talk, the agent's talk, and come in quickly.

"If you love the Comanches . . . who, by returning to the bad road after Washington gave them back their women and children, made it hard work for you to get back Satanta and Adoltay . . . more than you love your own wives and children and so stay out and miss getting your annuities, the loss will be yours, and you cannot blame the agent for it.

"The road you used to travel was a bad road . . . you killing white people, white people killing you in return. It is because Washington wanted a better road made that he sent you better agents.

"Your agents used to get drunk, act foolish, steal from you. Now you have better agents who do not get drunk or act foolish or steal from you. We do all we can to keep the Indians on the good road. Is that not so, Kicking Bird?"

Kicking Bird looked up from the fire. His countenance had changed. Battey knew that he had been with the Cheyennes and Comanches. He had heard their talk. Their words had given him a wrong impression. He had been angry even with Thomas Battey. Now the storm had lifted.

"I know the Comanches have been raiding in Texas. Now I want to ask you a question, Thomas." The Quaker became attentive to Kicking Bird's next words. "Had we better go in and get our annuities, or stay out?"

Thomas Battey knew that the annuities were not the issue. The camp was full of fresh buffalo meat. There was food, and there were robes for trading. Kicking Bird was in a soft way putting the question of peace or war. Going to the agency under the circumstances with the Comanches would show that the Kiowas were determined in their friendship toward the whites. Remaining out would indicate their sympathies were with the Comanches.

"The agent will not bring your annuities to your camps, Kicking Bird. He tells you that you can have them by coming after them. I think you had better go and get them. The agent's heart is warm. He does not want any trouble to arise. But he is alone. Perhaps, if his Kiowa friends come in, they can help him stop this trouble, even after it has begun, so that it will not amount to much."

"Guit-ar-ke to-zant, Thomas," the men around Kicking Bird's fire said. "Thomas's talk is good."

Kicking Bird tossed a small stick into the fire. "We will take your advice and go to the agency. I will make my camp and sit down where the agent tells me."

Chapter Twenty-Five

"The Kiowas had decided to make peace," Daha-hen continued his story. "Kicking Bird had led the way, but many of us were thinking about the peace road. It beckoned to us with good sense. Our chiefs were home, unharmed, and had been treated well. We knew the Comanches were fickle and heading for trouble. But even among them it was only a few who would not give up the old ways that were getting them in trouble. They were heart-torn, wanting peace, but not wanting to turn over their children."

"I do not understand what all this has to do with Kicking Bird's death. You said he was for peace. You said he saved your life."

"You will understand eventually." Daha-hen pulled up his pony and dropped to the ground. "*Ahe!* Here is where they camped last night. Get down, boy. Do not take my word for it. Look around you. See, learn, feel the ashes in their fire. Here is an empty can. Here they scraped out their plates."

Thomas went over the site with Daha-hen. In the twilight he was able to discern the different tracks of five men. He knew what they had eaten, where each had slept.

"They did not even post a picket," Daha-hen observed. "They just left the herd to itself." He added gleefully as he returned to his horse: "I like these white men. They are wonderful fools. It is more challenging to deal with a subtle or cunning enemy. But it is refreshing and effortless to catch such fools."

"It will not be so effortless, I think, when we meet their guns," said Thomas.

"You are a worrier, Thomassey. I have told you fighting is not just weapons but your will. And I will to have my horses back."

Daha-hen remounted and trotted on, resuming his story.

"Pay attention now, Thomassey. I am getting to the good part. The previous winter had brought me to the edge of the peace road. Again, during the winter of Eighteen Seventy-Three-Seventy-Four in the white man's time, I sat down to listen. This was the winter Satanta came home. Satanta had learned many things about the white men while he was in prison. He had seen their ways. But he still thought that he could bring them to negotiate with the Indians by killing surveyors and buffalo hunters and the Army. He thought that what was needed was an alliance, a coalition of all the wild tribes to make combined attacks big enough to make the white men listen. He said we must all lay aside our personal revenge or raiding so that we could strike together at the kinds of targets that would show our collective displeasure.

"Satanta wanted his words to be true. I think he believed them. But I had seen the pictures in the stereopticon. I knew the white men would not be pricked by our displeasure any more than a rutting buffalo bull worries about a gnat blowing his ear. Satanta was not the only one going about the winter camps with this

192

idea. Indian unity was in the air that winter. The Osages traveled about talking of 'one mother, one fire.' By that they meant that the Indian peoples had one mother in common, the earth. We should therefore, according to the Osages, forget our differences and take council together at one fire. This was not well received by the Kiowas because we remembered that the Osages had killed our people and cut their heads off and put them in the cooking kettles in our camps. That was a very long time ago, but it colored our view of the words of the Osages.

"Among the Comanches a medicine man appeared who said that the Indian peoples were going to rise together and defeat the white men. This Comanche's name was Isatay, or Coyote Dung. It was a suitable name for any prophet but particularly so for this one. Everything he said was excrement. He said he could belch up cartridges for our guns, wagon loads of cartridges. He said his power would keep the Indians from being killed by the white men's bullets. They could shoot at us, but they could not hit us. This man had never seen a buffalo gun, I thought. He could heal the sick and raise the dead, too, he said. Many believed him.

"Isatay would cause a lot of trouble for the Comanches. But they were very mixed up from dealing with the white men. Sometimes the white men were good toward them as when they returned the Quohadi women and children. Sometimes they were bad toward them and wanted them to turn over their young men, or withheld food from the peaceful Comanches because of the raiding Comanches. They never knew which way the white men would jump. And, I think, for the first time they were afraid of the white men because they had been able to take their women and children. They had to watch the white men carefully. Trying to keep up with the white men had made their heads swim.

"And they had never had much dealing with medicine men. The Comanches did not have an organized religion like the Kiowas. Each man had his own beliefs and superstitions. Some beliefs they had in common, but they did not have a Sun Dance with Tai-me and the Grandmother god. It is still so with them. Sometimes in the summer they came to our *Kado*, but for the fellowship and food, not the religion.

"It is very hard to quit being a warrior when you have been raised to it, and it is the only life you know. I had that problem. Many men did. It seemed that something was missing from our lives. While I worked with my horses, other men went on raids, even though we had said we would not. They went to Mexico and left the Texans alone. This seemed satisfactory to us. We did not think Woosinton would mind what we did to Mexicans since they were not his children.

"We were going along pretty good. Even Lone Wolf had been satisfied after his trip to Woosinton and Satanta's return. He had told Battey he thought all the killing should be forgotten on both sides. If young men got killed on raids, that was a chance they took. Their families would have to endure it. Then his favorite son, Tanankia, was killed in Mexico. Lone Wolf forgot what he had told Battey. His grief was too big. Lone Wolf forgot what Satanta had said about personal revenge also. Lone Wolf did not care about unity or about the danger of fighting white men. He did not care about dying because his son was dead. He went to bury his son's bones. Coming home, he hit the horse herd at Fort Concho.

"The Comanches were very stirred up. The Army killed eleven of their men in a single fight at Double Mountain. The Cheyennes were riding about, stealing horses and cattle. When Little Robe's son got killed by the Army, the Cheyennes got even meaner. Little Robe had been friendly. But now he was like Lone Wolf. He did not care if he died.

"The Comanches and the Cheyennes were stealing anyone's horses who wanted to make peace and quit raiding. They wanted the Kiowas to join them. But Kicking Bird was holding the Kiowas. His two best horses and his daughter's horse were stolen. He was very angry that anyone would steal the little girl's horse, not to speak of his own. He went after them and took them away from the Comanche thief. If he had caught that Comanche in the open, he would have been a dead Comanche. Kicking Bird was not afraid of anyone, not even Satanta. In fact, I saw Satanta send apology gifts to him once so he would not fight him.

"But the Comanches would not let up on Kicking Bird. They did not steal his horses much anymore, but they harassed him wherever he went. If he moved his camp and herd so there would be more grass, two Comanche bands would follow him. Very quickly the grass was eaten up in that place, too. Kicking Bird would have to move again. They kept doing this, pushing him off the best grass toward the east of the agency. There his herd was easy for the Texans to reach and steal. The whiskey dealers were also close there. Kicking Bird's men would drink and get into trouble. This went on all spring.

"We could see the big American horses among the Comanche herds. We knew they had been raiding in Texas. We knew the government would take some action. If we were around them, we would get hurt, too. All together it put a lot of pressure on Kicking Bird. But he held to the peace road. I was now beside him. Among the Kiowas only Woman's Heart and Lone Wolf had taken the war pipe."

Kicking Bird came into the agent's personal office. Whenever he was camped nearby, it was his custom to spend some time in the evening in social conversation with Agent Haworth and Thomas Battey.

"How are your people making out?" asked Haworth. "I know you are short on rations. I've tried to get in enough, but I have failed at this point.

"We are not eating our bow strings yet." Kicking Bird then smiled. "We will last a while longer, but short rations will make people willing to listen to the Comanches and Cheyennes. They'll have a point that you aren't doing your jobs. And they'll make it. Every chief is not mad, Haworth," the Kiowa added. "I feel good in my heart because several Comanches, like Horseback, have brought in stolen stock. The raiders ask a high price for those horses, but he will pay it from his herd so he can bring them to you, so there will not be trouble."

The agent paced in front of the window. He seemed deeply troubled. Kicking Bird tried to help him. "I have not smoked the pipe. Even many Comanche chiefs are tired of it. I have a little son now. Thomas has given him a white man's name . . . John. He will join my daughter on the peace road."

Outside the office the Kiowa, Running Wolf, slipped into the shadows that hid the door. He rested his head against it, listening.

"What do you think will happen with the Comanches?"

inquired the agent of Kicking Bird.

"I believe that many of the Comanche chiefs are like me. We are anxious to do right and to have our people do right. But there are many young men who will not be controlled. The Comanche chiefs' only power is to move their camps away from troublemakers. This is getting very hard to do. But the men who do wish to do right are increasing. These troublemakers are only making us dislike them more as they push us to join them." Kicking Bird stood up. His visits were cordial but generally short, since he was on his way home.

Running Wolf scurried off the porch, caught his pony, and trotted away from the agency. He slipped from the horse some time later at Woman's Heart's camp. He immediately lifted the door of the chief's lodge and disappeared inside.

"Woman's Heart," Running Wolf spoke first to his host, "all of you chiefs gathered at this fire must know that Kicking Bird is betraying you right now to the agent. He has told him for sure that Woman's Heart has taken the pipe. But don't any of you feel secure. He is telling Haworth many lies about you, each of you. That way the agent will keep back your rations, and Kicking Bird's people will have more."

Woman's Heart jumped to his feet. "This time Kicking Bird has said too much to the white man. I will straighten this out once and for all time."

The ride to the agency did not cool off Woman's Heart — not with Running Wolf continuing his diatribe against Kicking Bird. The war chief hit the door of the agent's office in nearly a frenzy.

"You will not listen to that spy, Battey," he said, pointing at the Quaker teacher who was placing a book on the

197

agent's small shelf. Thomas looked up. The agent stood. "Kicking Bird has been lying about me taking the pipe. That is final. You cannot withhold food from us to give to that liar's people. Because he has lied about us so badly, we Kiowa chiefs have thrown Kicking Bird away. He will not influence anyone anymore."

Haworth walked around the desk to the side where Woman's Heart stood with hands on hips. "Kicking Bird has just left here, but he said nothing against anyone. He says only that the young men are difficult to hold. We already know that. He says that many chiefs are looking at the peace road. Let us sit down and talk, Woman's Heart."

"You are lying for Kicking Bird. His words have been heard." The big Kiowa chief turned to go. Haworth offered his hand. The chief ignored it and walked out.

Battey came to Haworth's side. "I fear that Woman's Heart has gone away to sow his wildfire in the camps of the Kiowas."

"You speak my thoughts," said Haworth.

The following day a messenger arrived from Woman's Heart. He and a group of chiefs were coming in to talk again to Haworth and get the record right. Haworth and his staff waited. When the chiefs arrived, they were all heavily armed. Entering the agent's office, they took seats around the room. Each had a strung bow and a cluster of arrows across his lap. Revolver butts protruded, uncovered and ready for easy grasping at each waist.

A noise outside drew the Quaker agent's attention from his guests' armaments. Kicking Bird had arrived. With him was his brother, Couguet, and Trotting Wolf. He tied his pony to the gate and walked quickly up the path and into the agency. Kicking Bird looked pleasantly around, noting those present and their weapons. He seated himself. With stoical coolness he and his companions placed their bows, arrows, and revolvers in the same positions as the others for convenient use should the occasion arise.

"Agent Haworth," said Kicking Bird, "these Kiowas say that I told lies about them when I visited with you last evening. I now want you to tell them what I said and hold nothing back. Tell my people my whole talk."

Haworth swallowed. Before him the room was a porcupine of Indians, waiting to discharge its quills. Haworth must speak thoughtfully. He must disarm this volatile situation.

"Well, Kicking Bird, I will certainly do as you request. There is nothing to hide, is there? Friends, Kicking Bird is an extraordinary leader. He has done more for his people than any other chief by helping them to take the peace road.

"Last night I did talk with Kicking Bird as a friend. He told me nothing that I did not already know. He said nothing bad about any of you. But even if he had, it would not have mattered, because I had already made my report to Washington. Daha-hen's words, made in council with all of you hearing, were the basis for that report. He spoke for the whole tribe, not Kicking Bird. So leave this anger behind you. Nothing has been done in secret. Kicking Bird and I talked as friends, as individuals. I did not take his words as the voice of the tribe."

Haworth glanced at Kicking Bird. The chief's head was bowed. Woman's Heart spoke.

"You took the words of Daha-hen as the words of the Kiowas?"

"Yes," said Haworth. "That is right. My official report

was based on Daha-hen's words. You all heard them."

The chiefs rose, following Woman's Heart. Each shook Haworth's hand and departed. Kicking Bird did not. Haworth frowned as the peace chief passed him with his followers. He watched him mount his horse and ride away. Not once did he speak to or look at another chief.

When Thomas Battey returned from his work at the commissary for his evening meal, he found Agent Haworth still pondering the day's event. "Kicking Bird left without shaking hands with me. That's the first time he ever did that."

"There must be something wrong," said Battey. "I'll talk to him about it."

"I think he's with his wife at the store," one of the clerks said. "He was going in as I left. I think they are pulling out tomorrow, and she wanted to get some things."

Battey glanced at Haworth, then laid down his napkin, and left the table. When he reached the store, Kicking Bird was sitting by himself in a dark corner. His wife and daughter were shopping.

"Why didn't you shake hands with the agent?" asked Battey.

Kicking Bird looked up at the slim Quaker standing before him. "He has thrown me away in front of my people. Woman's Heart has convinced them that I am a liar, so that they will not listen to me. And now, my friend, the agent has told them that he does not listen to my words but takes Daha-hen's words as the word of the Kiowas."

"The agent has not thrown you away," Battey said. "You misunderstand white men's ways. We regard some conversations as private, others as public. In general, we base our official reports only on what is said publicly. You misunderstand Agent Haworth's intentions."

"If I misunderstand, so has every other Kiowa that was

200

there. Daha-hen's words are now taken as the words of the Kiowas. Daha-hen is new on the peace road. For five years I have been walking this road, working to bring others to it. All these years Daha-hen has worked against me to keep my people on the old bad road. When I have brought in white captives to the agent, Daha-hen has taken more. Now for a little while he has come on the good road. The agent has taken him by the hand and thrown me away after many years of labor. He has taken up Daha-hen who is yet walking on the legs of a new-born colt. Can he carry the white man where he must go to have peace?

"I am a stone, broken and thrown away, Thomas. I am chief no more. But that is not what grieves me. I am grieved at the ruin of my people. They will go back to the old road, and I must follow them. They will not let me go and live with the white people. But I shall not go away on the gallop. I shall go to my camp, and after a while I shall go a little farther, and then a little farther, until I get as far away as it is possible for me. Whenever they show me the new chief they select, I will follow him."

Kicking Bird's young wife came to him, carrying the baby, little John. "I have made my purchases."

The beaten chief rose and followed her to the counter. He picked up several bundles and took them with the woman to the horses outside. He helped her place the baby's cradleboard on the saddle. The bundles he secured on the back. One he placed on his daughter's saddle. Sending his family ahead, he walked back and stretched out a hand to Battey who stood on the porch.

"Good bye, Battey," he said.

"Good bye, Kicking Bird," the Quaker said. "I, too, will be leaving here soon. If the Kiowas have thrown you *away, they have thrown me away also. My work here is finished. I can go back to my children now. Do you think our children will ever meet?"* The Quaker looked down, kicked the toe of his boot against the post he leaned against. *"I wish we could have made it. I think we could have, together. I never thought you could bring in Daha-hen, but you did."*

Kicking Bird sat down on the porch step and looked at the sun, dropping down on the horizon. The sky was a hot red like a thousand fires raging just out of sight. His wife and daughter and infant son were riding into the fire. "The sky is burning, Thomas. Pretty soon my wife and children and my people will be swallowed up."

The Quaker sat beside him. "It only seems that way. You took the good road so that wouldn't happen. Maybe it won't. Maybe Daha-hen or somebody else will hold your people on the peace road."

"Daha-hen can't do it alone," said Kicking Bird. "He has not fully taken the white man's hand. He's reached out, but he has not grasped."

"Shame to throw your work away, Kicking Bird. You are the only man I know who can bring the People into the good road. Agent Haworth knows that, too. I wish you knew it and would step up. Agent Haworth will always call for you when he wants someone to speak for the Kiowas. But if you will not come. . . ."

"Haworth will hear me as chief?" asked Kicking Bird.

"Who else, my friend? Who else?"

"I will go now to my camp, collect my band of people. You stay here and do not go home. I cannot take you with me now because, if they kill me, I could not save you. But when I come again, Thomas, you will know . . . everyone will know who speaks for the Kiowas."

* * * * *

On the sixth of June, 1874, Kicking Bird returned with Daha-hen and his people to the agency. He told Battey that the Comanches and Cheyennes were intractable. They were beyond his persuasion. He feared that they would not leave the Kiowas alone at their Sun Dance but would continue to incite them to violence. He told Battey that he would not take him along as he had planned. Lone Wolf had returned from Mexico where he had buried his son. He had made a vow to take a white man to the place where Tanankia died and kill him there. A white man in camp would be too convenient. Kicking Bird's white friend would be a great prize — a way of shaming the chief. Thomas Battey sat down to wait for his friend and his companion, Daha-hen.

Chapter Twenty-Six

Daha-hen chewed the jerked meat in his mouth. "The white men had given the Nokoni Comanche chief, Horse-back, an ambulance to travel about in. He was bleeding from the lungs. But when the Comanche prophet, Isatay, said he could heal all diseases at the Sun Dance, Horse-back brought back the ambulance. He and his women, the ones that had been held at Fort Concho, rode slowly toward the junction of Pecan Creek and the north fork of Red River.

"When they got there, the prophet had no time for healing. He was leading a raid. At first the Comanches and Cheyennes wanted to hit the Tonkawa scouts at Fort Griffin. But someone told the plan, and the soldiers moved the scouts inside. Then, somebody thought about the thing Indians hated more than Tonkawas — buffalo hunters. The plan changed to the buffalo hunters at Adobe Walls.

"That was an Indian mess. Quanah got his horse shot out from under him. The prophet's magic turned out not to be proof against bullets. Seven Comanches and six Cheyennes died and forty-six horses. Buffalo hunters can kill a horse from a mile away. When the Indians left, the buffalo hunters came out, cut off the heads of all the dead ones, and stuck the heads on the corral posts. There were thirteen heads still rotting there when

I cut across during the Wrinkled Hand Chase. Isatay blamed the whole failure on some Cheyenne who had killed a skunk on the way to the fight. That was enough prophecy for the Comanches.

"After that, there was nothing but fighting. Gray Bear, Stone Calf, Heap-of-Birds, Medicine Waters all kept up a steady stream of war parties. They surrounded the agency at Darlington, cut them off. Agent Miles had to send a man to Fort Sill for help. But before Colonel Davidson could get there, he got news of an attack on the Wichita Agency and had to go there. Miles broke out for Fort Dodge. On the road he found some dead teamsters the Cheyennes had massacred. Naturally, Woosinton wasn't going to accept that.

"The Cheyennes and Comanches moved their families up to our Sun Dance site. At the Kiowa Sun Dance we tried to stay away from the Comanches and Cheyennes. Lots of Kiowas could see what trouble was coming. . . ."

Satanta was in the center of the circle. In his hand was the Zebat, medicine lance. The other Kiowas knew the lance very well. Satanta had carried it since he had retrieved it from the spot where the Koitsenko warrior, Tanguadal, had staked himself and been killed. It was a sacred weapon, the symbol of Satanta's personal glory. He lifted it above his head. The men became quiet.

"You have seen this weapon. I have carried it for many years. I took it from a young man in a great fight that you all remember. In those days we, Kiowas, fought only for glory. The men we fought with, fought only for glory. Our deeds were told many times. Each of us wanted his name to be great.

"We did not think of anything but our own bravery and

205

glory. Many young men still think that way. But we canno
go on thinking that way. We must not fight as weak littl
fingers. We must close our fingers, our personal fights
into a Kiowa fist and strike together for war or for peace

"Kicking Bird and Daha-hen have told you that the whit
man is too big and too strong to hurt. They have tol
you that the Kiowa people will be wiped out if we figh
the white man. I do not want this to be so. But it ma
be so.

"Today, I am giving away the Zebat. I am giving awa
this symbol of my personal power." Satanta handed th
decorated weapon to Ato-t'ain. "From now on I will judg
a war path not for the glory it will bring to me, but fc
what it will bring upon my people. I want you chiefs t
think about this."

"Join us," shouted Gray Beard. "We Cheyennes hav
not grown old. We will offer you all the glory you ca
take. Ride with us against the white men. Show tho
you are still men."

Daha-hen stood up. "Many of you, Lone Wolf, Sun Bo
others have been to Woosinton. You have seen the whit
man's power. Many of you, like Satanta and Adoltay an
the Quohadi women and children, have also seen you
families reunited when you walked in the white man'
path. I think the Kiowas should continue on the goo
road."

"Daha-hen has become a woman," White Horse saic

Kicking Bird caught Daha-hen's shoulder. "Taunting wi
not help here, White Horse. Thought must be taken.
is one thing to throw down your own life. . . ."

"I will take many white men with me," joked Whit
Horse.

Kicking Bird continued. "It is another thing to throu

206

down the life of a people. These Cheyennes and Comanches are not Kiowas. They do not speak for us. They do not even speak for any Comanche or Cheyenne bands but their own. The Kiowas must decide what the Kiowas will do."

Lone Wolf pushed his way into the circle. "I am head chief of the Kiowas. I will fight. If you want to fight, come with me. You can find me with the Cheyennes and the Comanches. If you want another road, you must follow Kicking Bird who is walking beside the white man."

The council ended. The Kiowas finished the Sun Dance with heavy hearts. When the morning sun rose after the last day, the People packed their ponies and travois. Kicking Bird led his family toward Fort Sill. Three fourths of the Kiowa people followed him. Only Lone Wolf and Swan stayed with the Cheyennes.

These were the names of the hostile chiefs. The Kiowas were Lone Wolf, Swan, Woman's Heart, and White Horse. The Comanches were Mowway, Tabananica, Black Duck, Little Crow, Big Red Food, and White Wolf. The Cheyennes were Gray Beard, Stone Calf, Heap-Of-Birds, and Medicine Waters.

Whirlwind, White Shield, and even Little Robe, who had lost his son that summer, went to the Darlington Agency of the Cheyennes. They occupied three hundred lodges. Eighteen hundred Cheyennes did not return.

Lone Wolf, the Kiowa head chief who had lost his son, led his people in a revenge raid. Satanta could say nothing to stop him. He had given away his power. With blinding speed, Lone Wolf moved toward Lost Valley. He lured the Texas Rangers into a trap, killing two. Lost Valley was not far from the scene of the massacre of the Warren wagon train which Satanta had led three years before. The feeble efforts to stem the war had failed. The southern plains were on fire.

Mild Agent John Miles at the Darlington Agency had written to his counterpart James Haworth at Fort Sill:

There is no use talking, some of our Indians are on the warpath.

His simple words proved to be an understatement. By the end of July the Quakers had lost their battle for the Indians. President Grant signed orders, at General Sherman's request, transferring the authority over the tribes to the Army. In short order Sherman sent his orders from St. Louis to the departments of Missouri and Texas. The peaceful Indians were to separate themselves from the hostiles. They were to be enrolled by their agents, accompanied by Army officers. They were to remain near their agencies.

Thus Sherman believed he had removed the peaceful Indians from the battlefield plains and cleared the field for his commanders. He did not understand that Indian horses must eat, and that Indians could not sit down for long on the heavily grazed pastures around the agencies. He did not understand their fear of the Army. He did not understand that some were too proud to be enrolled and monitored by their enemies.

He proceeded with orders to his soldiers. Colonel Davidson at Fort Sill received orders on July 26th, transferring Indian management to the Army. He was told to begin the enrollment of all friendly Indians around the agency. He informed the Indians on July 27th. The enrollment began on July 31st. Agent Haworth accompanied by Captain G. K. Sanderson went to the camps. Horseback, now very ill, Cheevers, and Quirts Quip, these Comanche chiefs enrolled without difficulty. But among the Kiowas there was great agitation.

"By God, Haworth, you are coddling these Kiowas," Captain Sanderson said. "They had bloody well get enrolled and get it over with."

"If you persist, captain," said Haworth, "I believe you will drive them into Lone Wolf's arms. You cannot treat them thus. Give them time to talk, to think. Remove this onerous order to appear daily for a roll call. These men have come in freely. They have made a decision to follow Kicking Bird. But if you continue to demand, they will surely flee."

The captain threw the sheaf of papers he had been handed by the clerk back onto the camp table. "The Comanches have not made any fuss."

"Horseback is not able to fight. The Nokonis have left him. The other Comanches are either already broken men or long-time friends of the whites," the agent said flatly. "Taking the white road is new to most of the Kiowas. They are listening to Kicking Bird, going just a few steps, seeing if what he says about the peace road is true. If you insist on pushing them into daily roll calls, they will feel that they are not trusted, that they are prisoners in spite of their leaving their hostile tribesmen and coming here. What free man that you know would submit to a daily roll call? Ask yourself, would you?"

"They have until the third of August. Roll call will be on Thursdays before the rations are issued." The captain was gruff. He did not look at Haworth. "Colonel Davidson will agree to that."

* * * * *

Daha-hen left his horse at the base of Medicine Bluff and climbed slowly to the top. He stood looking at the plains. He turned when Kicking Bird came up beside him. "That is my country," Daha-hen said quietly. "All my life I have lived here. The wind and the grass smells are in my nostrils. The sun has burned me dark. My legs are bowed from the bellies of the many horses I have ridden over this country. No man is my equal on these plains. I know them. I can move on them. I cannot be found on them if I do not wish. I am a free man here."

Kicking Bird nodded his head. "My wife and children are buried on these plains. My ancestors are dust on the prairie wind. It blows them here and there, all around me."

"Do they not speak to you to come to them and leave this place?"

"They call to me as your fathers' call to you, Daha-hen. But they are not living. The time in which they rode freely, never knowing a white man, is past. Their voices are soft and far away from me. But when my son cries, he is very loud. He makes me forget my own heart. I know he will not live as I have lived. But I want him to live. I want John Kicking Bird to find a good life.

"If I fight the white man, I will lose. You have seen it in Battey's pictures. You know what is coming. If I am killed, no one will care for my family, no one will care for my people. Among our herds we have seen the mares and colts of the strong stallions. They have the good grass. Their colts survive. When the white man takes power, there will be no one to stand between them and the People if we are gone, no one to lead them in the dangerous path. They will be bowed down by bitterness and ignorance. They will be like the poor mares and dying colts of the weak stallions. Any wolf can take them. They will starve, outwardly and inwardly.

"I will lay down my life for them here. I will fight here, Daha-hen. Each day's battle will be a step farther down the road for my people. Some of the young ones will find their legs on the peace road. They will be strong men in the new ways if they have time to grow."

"Battey has gone," said Daha-hen. "You will be alone."

"I have found that white men can be dealt with. When I was a very young man, I was afraid to die in battle. My life was precious to me. I was very ashamed of my fear. My uncle took me aside. He said a man is born dead. What time he has between his birth and his dying is brief. And there are many things he must do. He must grow from a baby to a man. He must love a woman and make children with her. But most of all he must show that, though he is dying, he will not cower before death. A Kiowa does this by going into battle. Again and again he puts down his life. It is not the enemy he must fear, but his own unwillingness to accept his death bravely. When a man accepts his death, he can fight without fear. You have seen this. You know that such a man will live. A man who is willing to accept the death of old ways will live to find new ones."

"I cannot submit to the roll call, Kicking Bird. Your words are wise, but they are not written on my heart. I cannot lay down my life here. This road is strange to me. I still believe a Kiowa must be free in the old ways. I know we cannot fight the white man. I do not even want to fight the white man. But I do not want to be his dog." Daha-hen moved restlessly.

"Then you must go. This peace road is not yet your

road." Kicking Bird continued to look at the open endless prairie as Daha-hen went down the mountain and rode away. "The prairie is very old. And men are very young."

Chapter Twenty-Seven

With the arrival of Iron Mountain's Yamparika Comanches on August 8th, 1874, Captain Sanderson closed the registrations at Fort Sill. Lone Wolf, Red Otter, his brother, and Daha-hen's names were not on the record. All of the Quohadi and Kotsoteka Comanches and most of the Nokonis were absent. Sanderson placed the number of hostile Kiowas at between seventy and one hundred. Kicking Bird had held.

Satanta's name was on the roll. It was settled. He had taken the peace road publicly. He now settled down to enjoy it. He and many other Kiowas decided to visit the Wichita Agency on the Washita.

At the same time Big Red Food, hostile Nokoni chief, sent word to Colonel Davidson that he and some other chiefs were coming in. Davidson refused to accept him. He knew of his hostile behavior, and the rolls were closed. Big Red Food's presence at Fort Sill could only upset a moderately stable population. Big Red Food moved to the Wichita Agency, Anadarko. There he demanded "subsistence" from the Wichita agent.

Acting Agent Cornell refused to issue supplies to the intruders at his agency. They were not his Indians. They were not on his rolls. He did not have sufficient supplies. He feared trouble was coming because Lone Wolf was in the vicinity of the agency. Many of the Fort Sill Kiowas

were in his camp. Captain Gaines Lawson agreed. They
sent for troops.

Four companies of Davidson's Tenth Cavalry arrived
at noon, Saturday, August 22nd. Davidson crossed the
Washita into the agency grounds. There were many
friendly Wichitas, Caddoes, Pawnees, Delawares, and
Penatekas camped near the commissary. Big Red Food
had camped close to the Penatekas.

Davidson sent for Big Red Food. He told the chief that
the rolls were closed, that he had been given an opportunity to surrender and had not. Now, as a hostile,
he must surrender his arms and move his people to
Fort Sill. Tosh-a-way, a friendly Penateka Comanche,
persuaded Big Red Food to accept the terms. Lieutenant
Woodward and forty black troops of the Tenth escorted
Big Red Food back to gather his weapons.

The Comanche chief called to his men: "Come, and give
the soldiers your guns. We are going to surrender now
and go back to Fort Sill and sit down."

The men began to stack their rifles and pistols in front
of the young officer. He noticed that each brave was still
well armed with bows and arrows, tomahawks, and
knives. "Leave the bows," he said. "Just stack them
there."

Big Red Food pushed his way through the men. "We
cannot give up our bows. We need them for hunting."

"You agreed to turn over your weapons," retorted the
lieutenant.

"No." Big Red Food was adamant. "You send for Davidson. He knows we must have our bows."

"Why?" called out Lone Wolf. "Women don't hunt. You
Nokonis are women like the Penatekas."

214

Lone Wolf's men began to take up the taunt. The troopers began to raise their rifles as they stood in the midst of the pandemonium of taunts and cat calls.

The official record says that Big Red Food whooped, leaped to a pony, and escaped unharmed from a volley fired by the soldiers. Thomas Battey's journal recorded, from secondhand information he received from the Quakers at Anadarko, a different point of view. The Quaker wrote:

Big Red Food, desirous of a little council with another chief, mounted his pony, giving a loud whoop, to call the attention of the chief with whom he wished to speak. This was misunderstood by the soldiers to be the war-whoop, and he was fired at by the guard. Lone Wolf with his party, being near, returned the fire; thus a battle commenced, which resulted in the death of several citizens, the burning of several Caddo and Delaware houses, also the Wichita schoolhouse, the sacking of Shirley's trading house, with other outrages. The Comanches deny any hostile intention, and the fact of their surrendering arms before its commencement argues strongly in their favor, as it does not look reasonable that they would surrender arms on the eve of an intended battle.

Intended or not, the battle had begun. The friendlies were caught in the middle.

"God damn it," Davidson shouted. "Don't fire into those people." The black soldiers slowed their firing. Occasionally one still fired back at the circling warrior, Lone Wolf.

215

They eventually all responded to their colonel's orders. "Get these people out of here. Let's go. Move it. Move it. Fall back to the river."

Davidson did not willfully, intentionally with malice aforethought, massacre the peaceful Indians who had come for rations to the Wichita Agency in the big bend of the Washita. For two days he fought the hostile attackers who would destroy peace for everyone. He held the agency. When the fight at Anadarko was over, the Wrinkled Hand Chase began.

News of the fighting at the agency spread quickly, as the Indians fled away from the fighting, away from their hostile brethren. At Fort Sill the Kiowas packed up. The runners said that the Indians were being killed at Anadarko. The People were afraid the soldiers would come and massacre them. The place where the Kiowas had camped was empty. Only forty-four of Kicking Bird's people remained with him.

Kicking Bird had stood in the dust and watched the frightened people disappear onto the plains. The first drops of rain smacked into the parched earth. The rain came harder and harder, and still he stood. His daughter caught his arm and drew him into the teepee.

Daha-hen listened to the runner. He broke his camp and led his people west and hid them in a side cañon. He then rode back toward Anadarko. Sheets of rain poured down on him. Lightning exploded, filling the air with an acrid smell. Daha-hen rode on, defying the storm.

When he found Lone Wolf's people on Elk Creek, they, too, were wet. Their blankets could not dry, and their hands became wrinkled in the pouring wetness. Finally the rain stopped, then the mists lifted. The People looked out on the plains. A herd of buffalo grazed. The People were hungry. They must have food for the children, for the long journey ahead. The men organized a chase. Chasing the buffalo dried their rain-soaked clothes. They began to feel like men again.

"Anyone from Kicking Bird's band that is going back to Sill," said one of the chiefs as he rode among the women and men, butchering the fallen buffalo, "tell Kicking Bird we are going onto the Staked Plains, but we are not going far. When it is safe, we will come back, if he wants us to."

Satanta raised up from the carcass with his hands and knife still bloody. Kicking Bird was not among those who had fled. He was still at the fort, holding his faithful followers. Satanta knew that he was in trouble. The white man would not believe that he had fled in fear. They would put him back in prison. This time he would not get out. He wiped his hands on the grass and took his horse. "I am going to find the other chiefs," he told his women.

"We are going back," he told Daha-hen and Lone Wolf beside the waterfall.

"Wait," said Lone Wolf. "Stay with us. The soldiers are angry. They will forget, and you can go back then."

Mamanti, the owl prophet, was in charge of the talk beside the waterfall. "Stay, Satanta. The Kiowas must stay together."

"We cannot stay here," said Daha-hen. "The soldiers are everywhere. I have seen them as I have been riding about. I think we should move our people to safety, then we can go back and fight if we must. I have hidden my people. You can take these people with their buffalo meat back down Elk Creek. There is a cañon there in the broken

217

country that will hide them and protect them. You cannot take women and children onto the Staked Plains. I have seen soldiers everywhere to the west."

"Yes. Yes." The chiefs agreed. Lone Wolf and Mamanti remained silent. They followed the others back south along the east bank of Elk Creek. Scouts were sent north to read the country between the Washita and the Canadian.

In the safety of the Elk Creek cañon the warriors sat down to make their plans. "There is no reason that we cannot stay here," said Daha-hen. "The soldiers are to the west, anticipating our flight to the plains. If we stay here, they will overlook us. I will ride back to Kicking Bird and get papers that will let us come in."

"I thought you had left Kicking Bird and the peace road. Now you want to go back," said Mamanti.

"I did not want to be enrolled," Daha-hen answered. "I brought my people out to safety. We would have been unnoticed on the prairies, but you have started a fight. Now you have brought the wolves upon us."

"You are always going off." Lone Wolf spoke quietly. "When the Kiowas need you, you and your people are out somewhere, taking care of your own interests."

Mamanti held up his hand. "There is one way to decide this. I will ask the owl." The medicine man pulled the stuffed owl from his bag. He conjured and listened. The other men waited. Daha-hen paced in disbelief. "The owl says that we should go west. We will not encounter any soldiers if we go toward Palo Duro Cañon. We can sit down there in safety."

Daha-hen threw himself onto his horse. Satanta caught his leg. "It will be all right if the People go to the cañon. No one can find us there. It will be all right."

"That puffed up owl has never been right in my memory," said Daha-hen. "I will go and see what I can see. You follow the prophet . . . to your death." These last words he spoke under his breath as he rode away.

Daha-hen rode in a full circle around the plains. From a rise here and there he could see a hundred miles in any direction. He saw the soldiers moving onto the plains. He turned back again, heading up toward the Canadian. He found two young Kiowa men watching a supply train move slowly along the unroaded country. He rode back with them to the main party.

Mamanti and Lone Wolf stood behind a buffalo-chip altar. Mamanti's nephew rode forward to give his message. Mamanti placed a sage straw in his hair. The young man made his report. Time and again the young women whooped to encourage the eager warrior.

"You women be quiet!" Mamanti shouted at them, but his eyes sparkled. "Keep quiet. You will be the cause of some of these young men getting killed today. We must ask the owl what to do. Now, you men remember this, you must take off your shoes when you come to bring your presents to the owl and ask him what you want to know. At the waterfall he told me we would find soldiers walking on either side of wagons. There would be a great battle. Many men would have great honors. Come now and let the owl tell you about your destiny."

"We do not need to fight," said Daha-hen. "We need to get away. Some young men may hold the soldiers a while. But if we go quietly now, we will get away without a fight before they know we are even here. You have started west. Why do you stop? I have seen a way that we can cut between the soldiers if you say we must go west. But we must go now before things change, while there is still an opening."

"The soldiers will follow us," Lone Wolf said with authority. "They will hit us from behind while we are with the women. No one has seen any soldiers to the west but you. We all know they are behind us."

"They are taking those supplies somewhere," Daha-hen observed. "I think we should go west quickly. We can go many miles before they find our trail."

"Very well, Daha-hen," intoned Mamanti. "You take the women west. Lone Wolf and I will take the men east where the enemy is. The owl has said we will be safe at Palo Duro. There is no danger for us there even if the soldiers are there."

"There are soldiers there." Daha-hen felt the council was over. He was tired from his riding. He found some food and lay down to sleep.

"Don't you want to see the runs, the fights," asked Botalye, Mamanti's young nephew. "Today I am going to make four runs."

"Usually no one lives to make four runs," Daha-hen said, turning on his side.

"The prophet says I will."

"Well," said Daha-hen, "it is not possible even for Mamanti to be wrong every time. Perhaps you will live."

"You are a sour man," the boy whispered.

"I am a live man." The older warrior went to sleep.

Mamanti and Lone Wolf held Lyman's wagon train four days. Mamanti's prophecy was right. Many men took honors there. Fourteen men along with the dispatch riders at the nearby buffalo wallow all received Congressional Medals of Honor.

* * * * *

Mountain Bluff found the Kiowa camp on the south of the Washita. The People saw him ride in and knew that he had come from Kicking Bird. "Do you have a paper for us?"

"Yes," the Kiowa-Mexican said. "I have a paper signed by two officers and Kicking Bird. It will protect us from attacks by the soldiers." He reached into his shirt and pulled out a pristine white flag. "I have this flag also."

"Good," one of the women said.

"Take the flag and ride out to the soldiers," suggested one of the men who had been fighting Lyman.

"No," said the messenger. "I do not want to stop this fight. I have made no show. I want to smell some powder first."

The women and children began to cross the river when they learned that more troops had been sighted, coming from the west. Some of the men began to break off skirmishing with the troops and the train. It had been a good fight. They crossed the rising Washita to safety and began to push west toward the headwaters of the Washita, then intended to turn southwest toward Palo Duro.

Daha-hen watched as Yellow Walking Woman — beautiful Yellow Walking Woman, long black hair falling over her shoulder — received the child onto her back and began to climb. She never looked back. The other women followed.

He continued to watch them for a long time, then trotted his pony back into the village and toward the fighting. In a little while he saw the saddles and blankets that some of the Indians had abandoned to climb the walls. Some of Mackenzie's Tonkawa scouts were with them. They were looking for human flesh, not horses. Every victory for the hateful Tonkawas included a feast of Kiowa hands and feet and legs and arms, any part of their enemy.

"Heh. Heh. Heh-ah. Heh. Heh-ah." The sound of the death song came from behind a bullet-scarred rock. Poor Buffalo, the medicine man, lay back, singing. Red War Bonnet lay dead in his arms.

Tears ran from Poor Buffalo's eyes, as he looked at Daha-hen. "It is a great honor to be killed by an enemy. It is a great honor to die among your friends. Red War Bonnet is already asleep."

Daha-hen saw Red War Bonnet's wound. A single bullet had hit him in the forehead. Blood had run down on either side of his nose, into his blind eyes. The buffalo-horn cap lay beside him, but he had not been scalped. Only his little finger was missing. The enemy had cut it off to get the ring he wore.

Daha-hen rode over to the dead Indian's horse and caught its reins. At Red War Bonnet's body he gave the reins to a young warrior, the chief's son, and dismounted. Without words, the two men lifted the chief's body from Poor Buffalo's arms and lay it across the saddle.

Daha-hen led the horse slowly, followed by Red War Bonnet's son and Poor Buffalo, up the trail to the top of the cañon. There members of the dead chief's band waited. They stepped back as Daha-hen passed with the body. He brought it to Little Bear, Red War Bonnet's brother.

"Who will tell our mother?" the warrior asked.

"I will tell her," answered Daha-hen. "Where is she?"

Little Bear gestured toward his mother with his chin. "She is there among the women who have come up from below."

Daha-hen walked his pony slowly toward the women. He studied them as he rode. Ragged, torn, holding their children with bloody, cut hands they watched him. It was here with the women and the children, the men's hearts, that the soldiers had beaten them and would beat them again. No man could fight when his family was near. He would always think of them, of saving them, and not just of fighting. It was not so easy for a man to lay down his life when his woman was waiting, not for his glory, but for his strength. Such a man does not have the liberating freedom of abandoning his life. He has no mind when his heart is held with gossamer threads in beloved hands.

The women knew why he had come. He stopped his horse before the erect white-haired woman who had been, and always would be, the honored mother of the great chief, Red War Bonnet.

"Mother," said Daha-hen. "Your son has gone to sleep."

Elk Woman looked at Daha-hen's face as she spoke to the women around her. "Turn me loose. Give me back my knife. I am the mother of chiefs. I will not kill myself."

She walked slowly forward and lay her fine hand on Red War Bonnet's head. "This is my beloved son, killed by the enemy of his people." She lifted her eyes to the group of men who had followed Daha-hen. Poor Buffalo still held the buffalo-horn cap in his hands. "You, Poor Buffalo, I want to say something about your Grandmother god. Do not pray to it when I am sick. Do not hunt for something to cure me. I want to join my son in the land of Many Lodges." Elk Woman stroked Red War Bonnet's head. "It is a great honor for him to be killed by an enemy," she said strongly, proudly to his people. "It is what he would want." Her hand stopped

223

on his braided scalp lock. She bent to kiss the fallen warrior's head. She whispered softly to her son. "But my life is broken."

Daha-hen released the reins of Red War Bonnet's horse. Quietly he rode away. These were not his people, but he knew what they would do when he was gone. Little Bear would wash the blood from his brother's face. The women would dress him in his finest clothing. Poor Buffalo would reset the chief's buffalo-horn cap. The deadly wound would be hidden. And, indeed, the warrior would seem to have fallen asleep. They would dance in his honor. And, then, they would bury him in a hole in the cliff walls which they had climbed in fear. They would pile rocks over him. No one would ever know where Red War Bonnet slept, where he lay down his life.

Daha-hen sat for a long time. Finally he heard voices, laughing voices. Off to one side some Indians, members of another family band, had captured several Army supply mules. The mules carried only sugar in their packs. The young people were helping themselves to the sugar.

Daha-hen looked at the sky. It would rain again, he thought. Nothing important had really changed with Red War Bonnet's death or the death of the People. The rains still came. The wind still blew. People still laughed when they found sugar.

"After that I went back to Kicking Bird at Fort Sill," Daha-hen told Thomas Young Man. "On the way I found a woman walking alone on the prairie. I took her with me. She was Many Tongues who became my wife. When Lone Wolf and the others did not come in, Kicking Bird sent me for them because only I could find them. There had been enough fighting. Now there was just starving."

"Then you did betray the chiefs as Tafoya said," Thomas said.

"I went after the chiefs just as I am going after the horse thieves who took my horses." Daha-hen reined his pony to a stop. "There. Do you see that small speck of light?" The boy strained to see what the man pointed at. "That is their camp fire. That dark shape moving there are my horses. We can rest now a while. In the morning, while the white men are eating, we will show them our paper and get our horses back."

Daha-hen swung from the saddle as if he had not ridden for four days and nights. Thomas eased off his horse. Daha-hen hobbled his horse and tossed his blanket on the ground. "You could sleep, Thomassey. I will watch their fire."

"Did you betray the chiefs as Tafoya said?" persisted the boy. "Did you bring them in so you would not have to go to prison?"

"Here is what I did." Daha-hen spread his blanket and sat on it. The boy stood above him. "Come down, Thomassey. Here is what I did. I left Many Tongues with my mother and father and their band. I slipped into the reservation to see Kicking Bird. I asked him if I could come back. He looked at me for a long time."

"You have decided to lay down your life here?" Kicking Bird poked the dying ashes of his fire.

Daha-hen nodded.

"Lone Wolf and Poor Buffalo have gone out onto the Staked Plains very far. Someone must go and bring in these people. Will you go?" Kicking Bird asked.

Daha-hen nodded again.

"Good," the peace chief said. "Send in your people. They may sit down beside me."

"That was all he said to me. I asked him nothing more. I brought in Lone Wolf and Poor Buffalo. Your mother was with them. When we got in, the soldiers put me and the chiefs in the guardhouse. We were there many days. Finally Lieutentant Pratt came. He was to take the chiefs to Florida. We stood up. Kicking Bird came in among us with Pratt and other soldiers. He walked slowly, looking at us. Then he began to call out names. Lone Wolf, Mamanti, Woman's Heart, Bird Chief, White Horse, Double Vision, Zotom, Ko-ho, Pedro, and so on. When he had finished, he had not called my name. They let me go. I walked out of the prison and walked home to my family. Many of the other men were very angry. There was much strife among the Kiowas. Many men thought I had betrayed the chiefs. Pratt thought I had. He told the men I had.

"This time Kicking Bird laid down his life for good. He also let me go home. After the train had left, Kicking Bird sat down to eat. He began to have great pains in his stomach. They took him to the post surgeon. He died with the white men."

"Strychnine?"

"That is what I believe," said Daha-hen.

The boy turned in his blanket. "Do you think the white men are better men than the Kiowas?"

"I do not. They are just men, some good, some bad, some nothing at all. But they have done things with their minds. They have made great things while we were only living with the land and hunting and fighting. That

226

was life for us. Life for them is something else. They are not contented people. They are always questioning. How can I get from here to there faster, with less trouble? An Indian would get a better horse, but he would not think of anything besides a horse. How can I talk to people who are far away? An Indian would just go there and sit down a long time and talk a long time. But a white man will string a piece of wire and send clicks over it, and he will get other white men to understand. If a white man has a gun that shoots one shot, he wonders why it will not shoot many shots with less work. So he makes a better gun. An Indian will make himself a better bow, but it will still be a piece of bone or wood with a sinew string. It will still shoot only one arrow at a time.

"But I do not think the white man is smarter. We have learned to use the things he has brought. And it is in all men to observe and often wonder about things. When I was a boy, I used to look at the geese flying and think how wonderful it must be to see the earth from high up and to move so smoothly. But I never thought to do anything about it. A white man would. Their culture is made that way. It encourages such thinking among its best men. It is a different way of looking at things.

"I have always liked men who took action, men who did not bow to owl prophets. I have much in common with such men, red or white. I think a man can learn some useful things from them. A young man, like you, can easily learn from them. If you learn some from the Indian people and some from the white people, you should have a rich life, Thomassey. Maybe this is where you will lay down your life.

"Do not ever think to go back to the old ways altogether.

That would be foolishness. You must take what is around you and make a life. Nowadays there are many ideas to choose from. Even Many Tongues likes parasols and iron cooking pots. And when I was a warrior, I always took the best weapons the white man made and learned to use them as well as he could. Still, I never knew a white man that could use a horse as well as I can. Their culture does not teach them that. That is why I will catch these thieves and get my horses back."

"What if they fight you? We do not have the best weapons now," the boy thought aloud.

"Fighting and killing are not weapons, but will. A man can kill another man with a rock if he has the opportunity and the will."

Chapter Twenty-Eight

"Do you see that," one of the thieves asked.

"What the hell!" The Gambler tossed his coffee into the fire. "That son of a bitch, Daha-hen. He's needed killin' a long time. Today we'll put an end to that smart-assed liver eater."

Daha-hen held the paper from Agent Hall high over his head. The edges of the page caught the wind and folded behind his hand. He spread his fingers to force it wide, to make it visible.

"Can they see it?" asked Thomas Young Man.

Daha-hen rode steadily on with the boy at his side. The old carbine rested across his lap. Thomas gripped his own rifle tightly. He had put in all six cartridges before he and Daha-hen had started toward the outlaws' camp.

"Do you see that gully, Thomassey?" Daha-hen did not take his eyes off the scene in front of him.

The boy nodded. "Yes," he added.

"If they start to shoot at us, run for that gully." The words had no sooner been spoken than a puff of dust kicked up in front of the man and boy. The concussion came quickly. "I am glad the old buffalo guns are gone," Daha-hen said, and kicked his pony toward the cover with Thomas right behind him.

The *pop pop* of the thieves' guns continued as the

Kiowas leaned back against the bank. "That doesn'
sound like much," said Daha-hen to himself. "Just pis
tols. But they are coming nearer. We need to stop them
Now listen, Thomassey, you only have six shells. Yo
must not waste them. Be sure you can get a hit."

The trembling boy eased the rifle over the lip and reste
it. He aimed carefully as Daha-hen watched behind him
He squeezed the trigger. The bullet flew past the outlaw
and struck one of Daha-hen's horses.

"*Ahe!*" exclaimed Daha-hen. He put his hand o
Thomas's shoulder. "Try again."

The boy aimed again and fired. One of the outlaw
grabbed his arm. Daha-hen hit Thomas in the back o
the head approvingly. The outlaws ducked down an
began to wrap the man's wounded arm with a bandanna

"All right," said Daha-hen. "They are thinking abou
us. I want you to slip down this gully and come u
beside the horses and drive them away. I will draw th
attention of these horse thieves."

The boy moved to his horse and mounted quickly. Lyin
low over his saddle, he glanced back at Daha-hen. Ma
Without Medicine smiled and nodded to him. The bo
nudged the pony forward. Together they might have
chance. Alone he was not sure.

He stealthily worked his way down the gully and unde
the cover of the rolling land. Behind him he heard th
outlaws' guns popping at Daha-hen, who was tauntin
them, rebuking them for their stupidity.

"Hey, *tai-bo*, I know you can't steal horses," Daha-he
shouted in Kiowa. "Now I know you can't shoot, either
The pistols cracked. Daha-hen moved quickly to anothe
spot and popped up again with more words. "Thomassey
don't take all day. This is a little gully, and I am wearin

a trench running up and down."

The boy dashed over the top of the rise and rode straight at the shocked horses. Thomas had never yelled so loudly or rode so well. He was a Kiowa. He was all Kiowas.

"*Ahe!*" shouted Daha-hen when he saw the boy, driving the horses over the rise. He quickly jumped onto his small pony and sped down the gully and after the boy.

"What the hell!" cursed the Gambler. The thieves ran to their tied horses and rode hard behind the Indians. "I'm personally goin' to kill that son of a bitch."

"You're goin' to get the chance *muy* damn' *pronto*," his lieutenant shouted over the hoofbeats. "They can't beat us driving that herd."

Daha-hen looked over his shoulder. The white men were gaining rapidly. To escape with their lives, they must leave the horses. Daha-hen had ridden too far to do that. "Thomassey, hold up."

The boy turned his pony and rode toward his friend. "We must fight them," said Daha-hen.

"We are in the open, Daha-hen," protested the boy.

"Get down and use your horse for cover." The boy hesitated. "Now, Thomassey. Make your horse stand. Brace your gun on the saddle. Wait for your shot." The Kiowas dropped behind their horses.

"What if they shoot the horses?" asked the boy.

"Maybe they won't think of that." Daha-hen drew his knife. "They are horse thieves . . . maybe they'll want our horses after they kill us."

The white men thundered closer, pistols raised for the kill. Daha-hen retrieved the paper from his shirt and waved it broadly. The robbers came on.

"Hold that damn' horse out of my way," said the Gambler to his companion. "Don't shoot that pinto. He'll make a fine lady's horse." The five outlaws bumped against each other as they tried to flank the Indians and shoot them without killing their ponies. Daha-hen continued to wave the paper. The outlaws continued to pop shots off when they thought they had an opening.

The Gambler spurred around Daha-hen's pony. He pointed the big pistol straight at the Kiowa's head. He fought to steady his horse so that he could get off a killing round.

"I am going to shoot him!" yelled Thomas.

"Go ahead!" Daha-hen replied.

Thomas fired. The bullet caught the Gambler in the chest and knocked him backwards off the horse. His back was broken. He hit the ground with a thud. Lying facedown in the grass, with his arms extended into the air behind him, he convulsively discharged his pistol into the air.

Daha-hen watched the flurry subside. Then he stepped up, placed the muzzle of his rifle against the Gambler's head. He fired the single cartridge he owned. When he looked up, the other outlaws were disappearing over the hills.

Thomas stepped up to Daha-hen's side. He stood a long time, looking at the dead man. *So this is what it is like to kill a man,* he thought to himself.

"It is not much, is it?" queried Daha-hen. "A puff of smoke. A noise. There is nothing left of the man but meat. A man is born dead . . . a long dying ahead. That is what the old Kiowas believed. A man only had the choice of dying well. This one died with his curse words in his throat, trying to steal a poor man's horses. He was not much man."

"Still he was a man," observed the boy.

"Do you want a scalp?" The boy shook his head. "He had a good jacket, but your shot blew through it. The blood ruined it." Daha-hen kneeled beside the corpse. He took the pistol from the ground and stuck it into his waist. He rolled the body over and jerked the pistol from the dead man's belt. He tossed it to Thomas who caught it with both hands. Daha-hen walked back towards his horse. "Let's go home, Thomassey."

As Daha-hen and Thomas rode through the camps along Elk Creek, the women shouted the men's names. The old Kiowas whooped and shot off their guns. "Thomas! Thomas!" the women cried out. The boy, son of Young Man, straightened in his saddle. His little pony trotted merrily along the side of the returning herd.

Loud Talker and his son, Broken Stick, and nephew, Gnat Catcher, watched sullenly. Broken Stick wanted to cover his ears. He could never call Thomas a *dapom* again. That was bitter. There would be taunting about his own return. But there was one useful thing. The horses were back. Tomorrow would be soon enough to ask Daha-hen about their horses.

Long before Daha-hen and Thomas drove the horses into Daha-hen's camp, Many Tongues knew they were coming. Elk rode out to greet his uncle and Thomas Young Man. Daha-hen threw his arm around the boy's shoulders. At the teepee he slipped from his saddle and drew his wife and children to him.

"Come down, Thomassey," the man said, looking up at the ragged, seated boy. "We will feast together as the old men did."

Thomas dropped beside Elk. The boys followed Daha-

233

hen and his family toward the arbor.

"The Methodists were asking about you," Elk said. "I told them you had gone with Man Without Medicine on his last raid. It may be, Thomas Young Man, that you are the last of the old Kiowas. You have laid down your life in battle and taken it up again. You are very brave."

Thomas said. "It was nothing."

"You are very brave," said Elk.

Thomas thought Kicking Bird knew that a battle was nothing but willingness to die, to do it well. Daha-hen had learned it. A man must lay down his life for something more than fading glory.

THE END

About the Author

Cynthia Haseloff was born in Vernon, Texas and was named after Cynthia Ann Parker, perhaps the best-known of 19th-century white female Indian captives. The history and legends of the West were part of her upbringing in Arkansas where her family settled shortly after she was born. She wrote her first novel, *Ride South!*, with the encouragement of her mother. Published in 1980, the back cover of the novel proclaimed Haseloff as "one of today's most striking new Western writers." It is an unusual book with a mother as the protagonist, searching for her children out of love and a sense of responsibility, rather than from a desire for revenge or fame. Haseloff went on to write four more novels in the early 1980s. Two focused on unusual female protagonists. *Marauder*, of the two, is Haseloff's most historical novel, and it is also quite possibly her finest book. As one review put it: "*Marauder* has humor and hope and history." It was written to inspire pride in Arkansans, including the students she had known when she taught high school while trying to get her first book published. Haseloff's characters embody the fundamental values — honor, duty, courage, and family — that prevailed on the American frontier and were instilled in the young Haseloff by her own "heroes," her mother and her grandmother. Haseloff's stories, in a sense, dramatize how these values endure when challenged by the adversities and cruelties of frontier existence. Her talent rests in her ability to tell a story with an economy of words and in the seemingly effortless way she uses language. Haseloff, whose previous Five Star Western is *The Chains of Sarai Stone*, once said: "I love the West, perhaps not all of its reality, for much of it was cruel and hard, but certainly its dream and hope, and the damned courage of people trying to live within its demands." *The Kiowa Verdict* will be her next Five Star Western.

THE WHITE WOLF
MAX BRAND

"Brand is a topnotcher!"
—New York Times

Tucker Crosden breeds his dogs to be champions. Yet even by the frontiersman's brutal standards, the bull terrier called White Wolf is special. With teeth bared and hackles raised, White Wolf can brave any challenge the wilderness throws in his path. And Crosden has great plans for the dog until it gives in to the blood-hungry laws of nature. But Crosden never reckons that his prize animal will run at the head of a wolf pack one day—or that a trick of fate will throw them together in a desperate battle to the death.

_3870-6 $4.50 US/$5.50 CAN

THE GALLOWSMAN

WILL CADE

Ben Woolard is a man ready to start over. The life he's leaving behind is filled with ghosts and pain. He lost his wife and children, and his career as a Union spy during the war still doesn't sit quite right with him, even if the man sent to the gallows by his testimony was a murderer. But now Ben's finally sobered up, moved west to Colorado, and put the past behind him. But sometimes the past just won't stay buried. And, as Ben learns when folks start telling him that the man he saw hanged is alive and in town—sometimes those ghosts come back.

___4452-8 $4.50 US/$5.50 CAN

Dorchester Publishing Co., Inc.
P.O. Box 6640
Wayne, PA 19087-8640

Please add $1.75 for shipping and handling for the first book and $.50 for each book thereafter. NY, NYC, and PA residents, please add appropriate sales tax. No cash, stamps, or C.O.D.s. All orders shipped within 6 weeks via postal service book rate. Canadian orders require $2.00 extra postage and must be paid in U.S. dollars through a U.S. banking facility.

Name_____
Address_____
City_____State_____Zip_____
I have enclosed $_____ in payment for the checked book(s).
Payment <u>must</u> accompany all orders. ❑ Please send a free catalog.

BACK TO MALACHI

ROBERT J. CONLEY
THREE-TIME SPUR
AWARD-WINNER

Charlie Black is a young half-breed caught between two worlds. He is drawn to the promise of the white man's wealth, but torn by his proud heritage as a Cherokee. Charlie's pretty young fiancée yearns for the respectability of a Christian marriage and baptized children. But Charlie can't forsake his two childhood friends, Mose and Henry Pathkiller, who live in the hills with an old full-blooded Indian named Malachi. When Mose runs afoul of the law, Charlie has to choose between the ways of his fiancée and those of his friends and forefathers. He has to choose between surrender and bloodshed.

___4277-0 $3.99 US/$4.99 CAN